I SHALL SIGN AS LOUI

I SHALL SIGN AS *Loui*

RHEA GALANAKI

TRANSLATED FROM THE GREEK
BY HELEN DENDRINOU KOLIAS

Northwestern University Press
Evanston, Illinois

Hydra Books
Northwestern University Press
Evanston, Illinois 60208-4210

Originally published in Greek under the title *Tha hypográpho Louí*.
Copyright © 1993 by Agra Publications, Athens.
English translation and translator's preface copyright © 2000 by
Northwestern University Press. Published 2000. All rights reserved.

Printed in the United States of America

ISBN 0-8101-1737-1

Library of Congress Cataloging-in-Publication Data
Galanakē, Rea.
[Tha hypographō Loui. English]
I shall sign as Loui / Rhea Galanaki ; translated from the Greek by
Helen Dendrinou Kolias.
p. cm.
ISBN 0-8101-1737-1 (alk. paper)
I. Kolias, Helen Dendrinou. II. Title.
PA5618.A295T4713 2000
889'.334—dc21
00-009945

The paper used in this publication meets the minimum
requirements of the American National Standard for Information
Sciences—Permanence of Paper for Printed Library Materials,
ANSI Z39.48-1984.

Contents

Translator's Preface — vii

Translator's Acknowledgments — xi

24 december 1888, patras — 7

25 december 1888, patras — 63

26 december 1888, patras — 77

27 december 1888, patras — 93

28 december 1888, patras — 105

29 december 1888, on the train — 133

30 december 1888, athens — 139

31 december 1888, athens, noon — 157

31 december 1888, on the ship, at night — 167

july 1897, patras — 177

Author's Notes — 193

Translator's Notes — 195

Translator's Preface

Rhea Galanaki was born in Crete in 1947, studied history and archeology at the University of Athens, and lives in Patras. She has published several books of poetry, fiction, and criticism and is considered one of the most important literary figures writing in Greek today.

I Shall Sign as Loui, her second historical novel, is based on the life of a nineteenth-century historical figure, Andreas Rigopoulos. "Loui" (pronounced *Louí*) is the pseudonym Rigopoulos chose to use in his correspondence with Edgar Quinet, a nineteenth-century French intellectual and political activist.[1] In the author's notes appearing at the end of her novel, Galanaki tells us that the title, *I Shall Sign as Loui,* is taken directly from Rigopoulos's first letter to Quinet.

Rigopoulos was born in Patras in 1821, at the onset of the Greek Revolution for independence. He studied in Italy, traveled widely, and became involved with the movement that aspired toward a European federation of free peoples. He died in the Aegean Sea in 1889, the year marking the one hundredth anniversary of the French Revolution.

Loui is primarily a man of letters, and he relies on the epistolary mode, relating his story and writing his apology in a series of letters to a woman he calls Louisa, who, according to Galanaki, is entirely fictional. The letters are all written during the last week of his life, but they span not only his entire life in and outside of Greece (in Italy, France, England, and America) but also the life of his ancestors and the history of his city, Patras, in the sea of which he was born. Louisa's narration constitutes the final section, the exodos.

Despite the references to history and the attention paid to geographical accuracy, *I Shall Sign as Loui* is not a typical historical novel. Interested in the question of what remains in and what is blotted out from human memory, and influenced by her training, Galanaki brings an archeological approach to history and to writing. The fragments from Andreas Rigopoulos's surviving works are the stuff she worked with in order to reconstruct a bygone era and a human life that has been more or less forgotten. These fragments are inserted in Galanaki's text and serve as reminders that her fictional world is an extension of the "real" nineteenth-century world and that art and life are inextricably intertwined.

Many of the fragments from Rigopoulos's writings are from funeral orations he had given for others. His death by drowning in the Aegean Sea deprived him of both a proper funeral and a funeral oration. Death by drowning, especially in waters far from one's native place, seems to guarantee obliteration from memory. Galanaki's novel stirs the lethe surrounding Rigopoulos's life and death, provides him with a sympathetic audience (Louisa), and allows him, in the figure of Loui, to give an account of his life and to record his disillusionments and his dreams. Louisa's contribution to the textual project, her narration and her function as the silent correspondent to whom Loui's letters are addressed, lends legitimacy to both Loui as an individual and to the life he lived. Her narration takes the place of the eulogy, lament, and epitaph of which Loui had been deprived. Louisa's words, like the words of so many women in both the literary and the folk tradition since Homeric times, attribute validity to his life and keep his memory alive long after his death.

By her style and method, Galanaki creates a doubleness that, as Roderick Beaton very incisively noted in referring to her first novel (*The Life of Ismail Ferik Pasha*), suggests a "rejection of the very idea of identity as single and undivided."[2] The lines separating the historical Andreas Rigopoulos and Loui are blurred, disturbing our neat categorization of truth and fiction and, in the process, compelling us to think not about the authenticity of the textual re-creation of a historical figure and the reenactment of a historical period but about such issues as memory and forgetfulness, identity and subjectivity, heroic dreams and human frailties, authorial enterprises and fragmented texts. "Fragments" in Galanaki's text assume extraordinary significance as they bolster the fictional/lyrical enterprise and connect it to actual historical events; but, at the same time, they remind us of the fragmentary nature of all writing and the fragility of human existence.

Following the original, translations of fragments from the surviving works of Andreas Rigopoulos are italicized and appear either in quotation marks or as excerpts.

Notes

1. In 1829 Quinet was given a post in the Peloponnesus. Upon his return to France in 1830, he published *La Grèce moderne*. He took part in the Revolution of 1848 and was banished from France for a time. He fled to Brussels, where he published *Les esclaves* in 1853. He died in 1875.

2. *Introduction to Modern Greek Literature* (Oxford: Clarendon Press, 1994), p. 292.

Translator's Acknowledgments

The translator would like to acknowledge and thank the colleagues, friends, and family members who have contributed in various ways to the final version of this translation: John Kolias, Aliki Dragona, Rosemarie Lavalva, Aldo Bernardo, Gonda Van Steen, Marian Rogers, Dora Polachek, Karen Maier Kolias, Josephine Perricone, Eleni Arvanitaki, and Steve Kolias. Although she is responsible for the content of the translator's notes, she would like to thank Rhea Galanaki and Aliki Dragona for their input and assistance.

Many thanks to the outside reader who made useful suggestions and to Rachel Drzewicki, Susan Harris, and Jacqueline Gecan of Northwestern University Press for their interest and enthusiastic support. Special thanks to Susan Betz, Amy Schroeder, Ellen Feldman, and Karen Keeley for their scrupulous work and many suggestions and improvements and to Rhea Galanaki whose good judgment, broad knowledge, and willingness to be of assistance made the process of translating enjoyable and worthwhile.

I SHALL SIGN AS LOUI

To Andreas Rigopoulos
(Patras 1821–Aegean Sea 1889)

24 december 1888
patras

Louisa,
This morning I stopped by the Phoenix, Panayiotis Eumorphopoulos's printing shop, and dropped off my literary and political writings that have appeared in published form during the last forty years in Patras, Athens, Zakynthos, Livorno, and elsewhere. My friend Vasilis Kalliontzis, by his own initiative, has undertaken the task of overseeing the entire publication of my works. I was able to locate and bring to him some unpublished texts as well. However, the financial difficulties are insurmountable. For this reason, he is considering enlisting subscribers and publishing my works in pamphlets.

One's writing should never be preserved as a whole, Louisa. With this in mind, at the printing shop this morning, I decided against parting with some youthful poems that I had composed in simple Greek at a time when brisk whiffs from the Ionian Islands still reached our shores. I am not speaking of the language only but also of the feelings. Besides, so many years have gone by since then. Some articles written in *katharevousa,* a language made necessary by the evolution of a certain type of reasoning and, at the same time, by the development of the new nation, were missing also—for the simple reason that I had not kept the clippings or the individual publications. Vasilis might inquire about them.

Not even for a moment did I consider handing over to the metal of the machines or to the harshness of the future the letters I sent my dear father from Italy during my student days. For the time being, I am also holding on to all your letters, Louisa. As I sit here all alone, I hear the effort of your quill on the paper. Most certainly I shall destroy them. As for the correspondence I had with Quinet, Hugo, Tommaseo, and others, I remember that I had given you their letters to safeguard when I was being persecuted and could not hold on to them. I hope you still have them. Vasilis may ask you for some; please give them to him.

Once again I wonder whether it was worth dedicating myself to the most pleasure-loving goddess of my days and taking time away from you. Would you be able to accept my ignorance one more time, after all that has taken place? Would you be able to accept this manuscript? Words, you might say, the words of one who had been a revolutionary and a poet, the traits of loneliness. You were reflected in both of these traits, which were not contradictory, even though your love was an attempt to pull me away to your own starry darkness.

Enough! I do not want to be carried away. The distance separating us will come to my assistance, I hope, as long as it does not become once again the most stealthy way of submitting to you.... Let my decision then come to my assistance. So tonight I begin this manuscript, rather too late for what I want it to accomplish. One way or another, it will arrive in your hands. My wish is that you destroy it after you read it.

I confess I do not know exactly what I want it to accomplish. It is not a report, because everything comes from such a distance and with such haste in my mind that it would be difficult not only to judge things but also to arrange them in a natural sequence. It is not a confession, since my way of thinking steers me away from anything of this sort, even though it did not deter me from embellishing my funeral and political orations with the most sincere and respectful words. Naturally, this does not have to do with my own funeral oration. As a public speaker, I know very well the traps of the genre, and I am unable not only to compose but even to think along these lines regarding myself. I am not referring only to our love: I am attracted not so much to what is concealed in a black-and-white sketch as to a painting's colors, when they allow me to bare the colorful image down to the outline of its conception. And if it is late for memoirs, it is equally late for an autobiography, a genre that I do not trust.

I want to write to you about my life: *"Memories waving in the ocean of the heart; feelings unceasingly throbbing in my chest; finally, a natural inclination of my soul and of my sadness. These stirred my reed to inscribe these words. . . ."* Incentives that moved me to a different type of writing in my youth move me in practically identical fashion now. Is it perhaps the moment when the image of youth reflects in the mature image the beneficence of one last vain and brilliant identification? Is this not also the fate of some ideas, of some feelings, at times when, between an end and a beginning, the weight of everything else becomes immaterial? To this immaterial essence I shall return.

The inversion of the hourglass, the rather scant sand that remains, could cover, up to a point, the blanks of a life, or of such a manuscript, if you would be willing to indulge me. I turned automatically to you, and I am not questioning my move. As soon as I named you, my words began to gush forth swiftly. But again, I feel that I myself am not in a position, not even with your name's springwaters, to seal my exposition and my posthumous reputation as a private citizen in the way that a work of art seals the exposition and the reputation of its creator as a public figure. So destroy these pages.

I write about the anonymous one, whom you had loved, having loved me. Don't be surprised that symbolisms of a whole lifetime—the lifetime of a romantic—compel me to remain anonymous. Furthermore, don't be surprised by the fact that you will also find your name changed here. Until the sand of this writing is used up, I shall call you by the name that I had given you once: I shall call you Louisa.

I start at the beginning, insisting on the logic of life and on the logic of narration, without ignoring, however, how sensitive the yarn of this straight line is to all sorts of winds.

I speak quite literally when I say that I was born on the sea. My mother's account of this event when we were living in Ithaca, where we had fled at the onset of the war, and my father's references to it gave me the impression early on that this was an extraordinary event.

Andreas Inglesis, the Cephalonian captain, had anchored his ship in the open sea opposite Dongana, the wooden structure that served as the customhouse on the more or less deserted Achaian seashore. Other ships were also anchored there waiting. People crowded the rowboats to reach them. Many dove into the sea fully clothed. Father helped my full-term mother on Inglesis's ship: he knew Inglesis well, having had business dealings with him in the past. Others also—merchants, elders, and landowners of Patras—had boarded their families on the sailing ships hailing from the Ionian Islands and from Galaxidi.

My mother gave birth on deck, surrounded by the mothers, wives, and daughters of these gentlemen. They gave her support during the delivery and at the same time concealed it behind the circle formed by their bodies—bodies made heavier by the multiple layers of clothing and jewelry they had put on haphazardly, having paid no attention to style or to good taste, as they tried to salvage whatever they could of their belongings. Still in shock from the turn of their own fate, these Fates talked about the events of the day over the newborn, forgetting that with these words they were spinning his future. They pampered the new mother who, resigned to her pains, resembled a country at the moment when it liberates its own future. It was a boy, a good omen.

Naturally, I do not remember. However, according to accounts of the event, the picture of homes burning on the fortified hill is what I first set my eyes on; and the sound of the frenzied ringing of the bells and of the shots from long-barreled rifles is what I first heard. For hours I had in front of me this first picture that the world presented to me, for the ship did not hoist anchor until all the colors had shrunk to black and red. The day after, ashes settled on the fugitives' blankets and clothes. Ashes were the stuff they touched—what was left of the substance of a lifetime: the leather merchant touched charred hides; the head of the household, a burned shaft; the landowner, a burned olive tree; and his wife, what remained of the art of lace making. Ashes also settled on my mother's breast.

Sleepless, the women spun tales around me all night, telling stories of drunk Turks who, on their way to the fortress, where they had been sent as reinforcements, dipped old rags in a bowl of raki, set fire to the liquor store, killed the proprietor, and attacked the home of a landowner. From there the fire spread to Patras. Our people, most of them Philikoi, and some from the Ionian Islands, took up arms and went down to the Turkish quarter, called Tasi. A battle ensued. As evening approached, the ambassadors of Sweden, Russia, and Prussia began to take refuge aboard the ships; only the ambassador of France chose to stay in the city. At that point, the citizens of Patras tried to save their families.

They said that the famous Androutsos happened to be on a

ship anchored near Dongana. A youngish captain disembarked with a few armed men and protected all those who were trying to climb up on the ships. It was the first time that his name became known. Decades would go by, and the then-young captain would call on me to give a public farewell for his dead son. He stood in front of me *"stripped of his position as general, poverty-stricken, bereaved . . . Makriyannis himself: a ghost."* These were not the only times we met, but I do not want to get ahead of myself, Louisa.

My father invited everyone on the ship to my baptism. It was to take place two months later in Ithaca, but the three names I would be given were made known then. The first was the name of the patron saint of Patras, the second was the name of the mythical king of Ithaca, and the third the name of a well-known ancient politician and admiral. Sniffing tobacco, my father then confided to the captain that, during her pregnancy, his wife had been in danger of miscarrying twice, as if it were not meant for his son to see the light of day in his parents' bedroom: once in December—when earthquakes had awakened the townspeople in the middle of the night, and, as they were rushing outdoors, they saw the frightful falling stars. His wife's agitation had lasted as long as the agitation of the earth, which kept on shaking for two days, bringing on hail and rough seas. The other time was earlier, when all of a sudden a small navy escort, accompanied by two cannon carriers, approached the coastline of Patras, looking for shelter from the weather. People were terrified, thinking that they were under attack—perhaps the captain still remembers the event. The commanding officer had handed out weapons to both Christians and Moslems and at the same time had sent word to Tripoli for military assistance. Very quickly Patras was full of soldiers—before it became known that the small navy was transporting the harem of Veli Pasha from Naupaktos to Preveza. The pregnant woman had been terrified, but not quite as much as the Turkish women, who, for the first time, exposed their confinement to the unchecked freedom of the north wind and the waves.

Reckoning that he could share a confidence, my father told the captain that his wife would have been further terrified if she had known that both her father-in-law and her own husband had been Philikoi for a long time. She knew only what she had to know: that both of them were landowners, merchants, and dignitaries of the town; that, years earlier, her father-in-law had come down from mountainous Kalavrita to Patras and had become successful in the currant trade, loading ships bound for Trieste and Livorno. Even back then the currant held a prominent place in the export business of the most important port of the Peloponnesus, although it had not yet exercised "its sorcery" like a "black-eyed Circe," as a local newspaper had written a few years ago—and I must confess to you, Louisa, I remembered the night of your eyes, for we had not seen each other for a long time. . . .

I sit here tonight and write to you about ancestors. I know that the longer the dead keep silent, the more likely it is for one to take the path of myth to find them. No words about a finished love affair come close to describing the dead's demise: perhaps because of the privilege of greater distance, of their unique relationship to us, but also of the freedom a closed world takes on in the mind when it is to be re-created. I do not object; many times these are the reasons that lead to discontinuity or break with descendants. By the same token, the contemporaneity of those in love is likely to do harm to the myth of their love, but, for the time being, I shall not elaborate.

In a few words, the longer a lost face gravitates toward its myth, the more abstract it becomes, while its shape is dissolved in the haze of the irreversible and the different. Here I would add one further thought, Louisa: that with the passage of time the dead become better and better, like a battle that is commemorated by a date, a place, and two names, despite its unbelievable horror. I am glad that, even at this late date, I can reflect on them calmly—although I shall never become familiar with them in the way and to the extent that I have been with you.

Why do I link you with them now?

My grandfather became quickly well-to-do and sought to marry the daughter of an old and wealthy merchant family. He had already become associated with her brothers, who used to ship currants to Italy and had established one of the first trading companies. If one is to believe what people said, until the time of Kapodistrias, the bride's family was the only one in town that was using the chamber pot, and the men of the family stood out among the natives because of their Western dress and their top hats. People contemplating their wealth added that only they, in all of Patras, began their dinner with mallow greens or beans and then continued with their regular meal. People said that they had voracious appetites, and they were often spoken of in connection with fantastic pagan symposia.

When I was young, I used to place the already wealthy grandfather and his always wealthy wife, whom I had never met, in the town of eighteenth-century Patras, which I also never saw since it was burned down during the Revolution. An imposing carriage took them to inspect their vast vineyards and proceeded with great difficulty on the dirt roads of the flat country between the sea and the town on the hill. The valley was full of marshes, and the carriages were in danger of going off the road near the vineyards and sinking in the ruins of the splendid Roman city that was buried there. Later on, in its marble and brick, would be rooted the marble and brick of the postrevolutionary city of Patras, of my city.

At other times, I placed Grandfather in Dongana, counting the sacks of currants that were put on the boat and later loaded on the caïque that waited in the distance. Or I imagined him walking with his wife on the cobbled narrow streets of the town surrounding the fortress, both looking flushed in the light of the low lying sun. Their forms darkened somewhat when they passed beneath arches of ivy and vine that popped out of the high stone fences around the individual homes. Other times, I imagined them promenading in their orchard: Grandfather playing with a lively dog and his wife, still young, bending to smell a rose with the nonchalance common to the slight movements of beloved women. The sea always appeared on the upper left corner of the picture that these literally untraveled ancestors sent me. In its bluish tint, a small ship raised its horn of plenty, which was as big as its old hull.

In those years, the coastal road was safer for trade, and Patras was one of the best-known cities of the East because of its commercial importance. Nothing seemed to threaten the coastal road, while the overland road, which cut through the Panachaiko mountain range before reaching Arcadia, had of late been named the Road of the Assassinations, a name which no doubt could still apply to many overland roads today. So my ancestors enjoyed all the privileges that their money and their associations allowed. In some ways, they were nobles. It seems that the nonexisting titles of nobility in Ottoman Greece, which, however, were used in the neighboring Ionian Islands, had been distributed quietly to the most important landowners and merchants, who, at the end of the century, had become, to a high degree, autonomous from the Turks. Simultaneously, the workers had begun organizing their own trade unions. Neither the former nor the latter, however, disputed the power of the nine consuls and vice-consuls, especially in these circumstances—even though they protested against the *miserrissimo consolato,* even though once in a while they unburied very old expressions, such as *mandare a Patrasso,* which meant that someone is sent to a place to die, or *andare a Patrasso,* that someone is on his way to his extermination. These were anachronistic expressions, the creations of a period when Venice exiled dangerous and corrupt men and those condemned to die to the region of Patras, so the fevers of the marshes would finish them off. These ambitious Greek merchants were not afraid of the "Europeans' Grave"; perhaps they hoped that the waywardness of the land would lead them more surely to riches, since they had learned the modern way of trading from the Europeans sent to the region, before the latter had died off. Furthermore, they knew, better than the foreigners, the products of their land, and, most certainly, how to bribe the bey. They also displayed greater resistance to the fevers.

I doubt, Louisa, that Grandfather accompanied his wife around their land or on visits more than a couple of times. I must write that in between the foliage of my imaginary Arcadia, where she is suspended (her light-colored silk skirts lengthening the movement of her suspension), I slowly learned to distinguish the bright eyes of the three spirits that accompany her: arrogance, ostentatious display, and indifference. People used to say that she made many attempts, although unsuccessful, to convert Grandfather to Western dress, top hats, and the use of the chamber pot. She realized early on that habits demand two generations to bear fruit and that money is not the magic stick that, upon touching someone, makes him instantly forget his upbringing, especially if his upbringing is in keeping with the general climate. Grandfather did not want to go down to Dongana in Western dress. Economic soundness demanded that he be unswerving in his appearance. His protests ended in time, before the advantages that were tied to the bride's family became threatened, without ever giving in, however. Besides, he respected the behavior of her relatives, which the boatmen of Dongana might have ridiculed. Her own people, however, forged a union between the good traits of the foreigners and the restless native spirit.

Restless, as if pregnant with a wild animal. Grandfather's

decision to move out of the shell of a mountain community and to very simply leave himself open to the fascination of business was a sign that times were changing and allowing him this smooth sailing. I am of the opinion that he was summoned not only by the fascination of business but by the prospect of the only solution as well. The simple logic of his decision rested more or less on the observation of, and the wish for, the advantages which the independent European nations had, not only in business but in every other area as well—although he was aware of the Westerners' harshness, which they did not fail to display, both as conquerors and as businessmen. However, now there was the matter of liberating the land. The old bloody ways had to be better coordinated this time with money and support from Europe.

My grandfather and my father became members of the Philiki when it branched out into Ottoman Greece. Many Patras merchants joined this secret society, which functioned as a further binding web among them. In joining it, they risked their lives, and they knew it. As a last resort, they relied upon their proximity to the ships and their connections in the Ionian state and in Italy. Most of them were self-made men, so they had the courage to become ruined and to start over again—to start over two and three times, if need be, knowing that business demands alertness and steady nerves. They had also prepared themselves for the possibility of sudden flight, having entrusted large amounts of money to Greeks abroad. As for their duties to the Philiki, they had to do primarily with giving monetary support and bribing the Turks. Secretly, they readied their own armed corps. When the time came, they showed that they were brave fighters.

"To the Greek merchants everywhere," Louisa, I dedicated the funeral oration for Pantelis Fakiris, which was given in the cemetery of the city of Patras about fifty years after the Revolution. I was also getting old. A few days ago, as I was arranging my papers before taking most of them to the printer, I looked once again at the text of my speech, which had been printed at the printing shop of Panayiotis Eumorphopoulos. I shall not disagree even today with what I said about the days before the national uprising and about its high priests: the clergy, the klephts, the merchants, and the sailors *"who promoted the transportation of ideas and of products and contributed to the enlightenment of the people with schools and with books; and, finally, the scholars, who were not pedants."*

It does not matter if all these things have been lost, more or less; before its fall or its oblivion, human beauty was accessible to the five senses. That is why I describe to you old times; and I return to the point where I had stopped.

Their daughter, my father's sister, set out with a marriage contract attesting that the bride was accompanied by a large vineyard, chattels, clothing, and a thousand kurus. Obviously not for a sea journey, but in order to continue the overland journey of her life, married to the chosen bridegroom, who was the offspring of an illustrious, equally old family. It had given a leader to the Orlofika, a man who was immortalized in an eighteenth-century text as "one of the most eminent notables of the Moreas, the most zealous patrician." Quite a few from this family had become members of the Philiki: one of them gave three thousand kurus on the eve of the Revolution.

My grandmother died later on during an outbreak of malaria. Grandfather did not neglect to follow along, after a short delay, and, as a result, he was not in a position to convey to her the news about the Revolution and about the simultaneous birth of her grandson. My father kept the family's landholdings and the business, converting the greater part of it to the leather trade. He did business with Livorno and Trieste. But during the course of the War of Independence, he became ephor of the Achaian Directorate, which was in charge of governing the place for a period of time, using its own flags, stamps, and emblems. Great sums of money passed through his hands. Later on he was glad that he had preserved these records. When I got a little older, I remember him showing me the register. He used to open it up and read to me the loans and the financing of the war. My mind used to wander off to priests and psalms. As I listened to the monotonous enumeration, I saw his hand petrified on the heavy book, and only when he turned the page did it become once again the white hand of a record keeper: to the Turks just before the war, 200,000 kurus (to throw them off guard, he would whisper to me); to Kolokotronis in Zakynthos, on the eve of the war, 10,000 kurus; 3,000 kurus to the Etairia; and the same amount to a Greek in Smyrna; three storehouses of foodstuffs and leather goods worth 10,000 silver coins to General Sisinis in Gastouni; 2,000 silver coins to Commander Zaimis. . . .

In retrospect, I cannot tell if the short ceremony had any other meaning than the initiation of the son by the father into the affairs of our country. The words of the register confirmed the mission that I believed had been imposed upon me with the clarity that natural phenomena have at the time when a tragic king is born in fairy tales. Did I believe in this mission, or did I simply want to abandon myself to the closed form of the fairy tale, to the hive of a very ancient pleasure? As an educated young man, I would reflect on my exception from the rule as an honorable curse—the doings, perhaps, and the excesses of youth?— and on my life as the search for an endless catharsis. I want to say, Louisa, that, after some years, I was also initiated into secret societies, following in some way an ancestral tradition of patriotism—with the exception that both the stage and the actions had changed drastically in my time. I do not deny it, there was always something that seemed persistently stable, but at the same time persistently unstable, transformed. I have difficulty describing it more analytically; nor is it imperative that I do so.

I am rattling on. I bring this paragraph to a close, Louisa, by laying down my doubts that my grandfather or my father would be able to regard my actions as a continuation of theirs. But I do not ask what exactly the word "continuation" means for each one of us.

We had returned from Ithaca. I was about ten. One afternoon, my father took me up to the fortress, and we sat under the plane tree. The old tree still stood outside the walls. Only it had been spared when the Turks set the town on fire. One night, twenty years after that particular afternoon, the fury of the winds knocked the tree to the ground.

It had been spared from the fire to give shade to the spring where marble spouts spurted water from the reservoir. Also, to spread its shade over the terrace in front of the spring, from where one could have a broad view of the lush green valley below and of the sea. The Turkish dignitaries, most of them connoisseurs of beauty, used to gather here in the old days. They sat cross-legged to discuss urgent matters, ordering coffee and narghiles from the neighboring coffee shop. If the clarity of the sky, the prophetic rustling of the leaves, the whispering of the waters, and the strength of the coffee or of the tobacco did not contribute decidedly to making the most advantageous decision, the proximity of the old Turkish cemetery definitely must have contributed to it.

Father looked around as if he could not believe that conditions older than his memory and stable for centuries had come to an end for always within ten bloody years. If only a spirit would return to the mnemonic waters of the spring to demonstrate to his son the hazy picture that he was describing! Taking tobacco from the pouch that he had filled at the tobacco mill on the way up, he turned to me all of a sudden and said, "Remember this: at one point we came close to losing everything, not only the profits from trading. That's how it all started."

And, as he smoked, he began talking about the ships of the North that paid cash at this marketplace of the Moreas; also about the European handworks that arrived in big piles in Dongana, to which people alluded when they said later on that the English had made Patras their warehouse: dark red fabric called *scarletina,* painted utensils, golden fabric called damask, plain solid-colored felt, fabric from France and Venice, chandeliers and expensive mirrors, crystal and hardware from Trieste, wax fashioned into tapers, French sugar, ropes, pepper, American coffee, hemp, hats of all kinds, combs made of ivory, baskets, pewter, lead, medicine, paper, and Greek books. The merchants of Patras sold them in neighboring towns and sent to Europe local products: silk cocoons, wheat, oil, cheese, wool, linseed, acorns, cotton, tobacco, rice, olives, citrus fruit, and especially currants and hides. After the Orlofika events, Patras and its merchants acquired privileges, and the foreigners acquired protection. Ships were not allowed to pass through the straits of Rio toward the Corinthian Gulf—people said that this was the case during the Roman occupation also—and this policy guaranteed great profits for those trading in the port of Patras. The French and the Italians controlled all the wholesale business (leaving only the wheat trade to the Turks and the Greeks), but they were soon sidelined by the English. The merchants addressed one another as "most honorable." But then the war that the sultan declared against the pasha of Ioannina almost destroyed them. The sultan's expenses were huge, or that is how they were presented. They were forced to take out mortgages or to sell without profit in order to pay the new taxes. The time had arrived. "Let us go to sleep with the Turks, but let us wake up with the Greeks," people used to say. The hour had struck; let everything go to ruins.

His voice had the metallic ring of a difficult decision. His glance was lowered to the shore, hesitatingly, not finding anything to rest on.

You were born in Zakynthos, Louisa, after our family returned from Ithaca to the Peloponnesus. When I later met you, I fished in your words for the sounds of my childhood years, words that sounded almost musical. Besides, my mother hailed from Ithaca, which is why we fled there when havoc broke loose. This was the reason, perhaps, that once in a while, after I became a grown man, I imagined that we were playing together as children. This could not have been, since approximately ten years separated us, and you had grown up on another island. I dare say that once, when I fell and was bleeding, you came, hugged me, and promised to marry me when we grew up. But you married someone else. There were times when I could not forgive the breach of a promise that could have been kept.

You often told me that you wanted to escape your real name. No word served to define you, since our love liberated you from everything that possessed you up till then—in order to deliver you to the most liberal bondage, I had thought, as I fell silent. You asked me to baptize you with a name that only the two of us would know. You could not have found a more clever way to move into my untrodden space. It was then that I named you "Louisa." I remember correctly: it was August—not only because your lips were like grapes but because at about the same time I had also found for myself, for undercover activities, the pseudonym "Loui." We were bound together by the ring of a pseudonym; we never exchanged any other. Our love was a type of conspiracy, a short story within irredeemable history.

Forgive me, Louisa, for a matchless—and, precisely for this reason, allowable, perhaps—trivialization of certain sentimental motifs. I am late in writing to you what I am now undertaking. Forgive me also, if you can, for the lyrical mood which came over me when I saw that I had no other way of speaking about Mother except by writing about you: both of you were an expression of excessive tenderness. Seeing that I am at the mercy of time, I would also like to beg you for something else:

that the two of you symbolize my emotional attachments as an immature young man and as a grown-up—since both of you were symbolic, in the way that an idea happens to take shape and to beautify our life, even if, in no time, it asks to have the gift it granted returned, innocently, as a small child would ask.

Let her remain anonymous and you pseudonymous on these pages—my gift to both of you in return for your caress—or for your voice, a voice from the past, sensitive, the horn of fair sea weather.

"*My hand dragged me along where I had not intended to go.*" I return, Louisa, to the events to emphasize that the ship of homecoming was definitely not the ship of the refugees. That can happen only in fairy tales, if at all. I confess I never understood where such a significant event stops and where its narration begins. In Ithaca I sat and waited for that ship to appear on the horizon of the wide gulf, the ship that people said had shielded my birth but at the same time had stripped the grown-ups of their previous life. It used to come to Ithaca whenever conditions allowed.

I used to watch it as it approached the shore and dropped anchor, thinking that I was waiting for someone close to me, made of wood, ropes, and dimity. At times, when it was anchored and the wind was blowing, I tried to hear the crying of a newborn in between the clamor of the rigging and the uproar of the waves. I never heard it distinctly; so, apparently, the great danger had passed. Once in a while the captain would take me on deck: wood, ropes, and dimity—was he the one? At any rate, he used to talk to me about old and recent battles and about numerous Greek victories. However, the sirens had been terrified and had hurried back to the palace of their father and king in the depths of the sea. The time would eventually come for me to see them and perhaps to love them, as long as things turned out favorably.

When the time came to return, I was eight. I knew the ancestral town in a roundabout way since grown-ups used to talk about it as if they were referring to their father and king, to their patriarch. Its body's memory was perpetuated in its descendants and its sacredness in stories that took on a different form day by day. Even though the years spent in Ithaca were in reality difficult, the return rewarded the grown-ups with justice. I was envious of it when I understood, as I was growing up, how difficult it is to grant catharsis in any drama. A poor shadow of it was my triumphant return from Italy to the port of Patras after Othon's dethronement. I hope to have time to write to you about it. As a child, I took part in the incomparable hour of homecoming, probably not because of my awareness of time (which was the privilege of the grown-ups), but due to the vision of what was without doubt a literally magic picture, because in between the tears, the stretched-out arms, the faintings, ourselves—young children then—overtaken by crying, we saw the unseen homeland.

Tall mountains. A fortress on the approaching hill and ruins all around. The verdant contact of the land with the water.

Since then, the archetype of melancholy.

Once, I saw a painting, painted by Admiral Wear, aide-de-camp of Lord Nelson, fifteen years before the Revolution. I can say that this painting contributed in giving me the most reliable picture of the ancestral setting that had framed life before me.

The admiral had painted the Panachaiko range, very tall and snow-covered, protecting the township of Patras, lifting it from the seashore that in previous centuries had been dangerous. Although the danger had dissipated at the time of the depiction, most homes had remained perched around the fortress. The sides of the mountain went down to the sea, forming successive triangular hills. An insistently verdant outline flourished at the union of land and water.

Big houses, minarets, domes—the town appeared to be

densely populated and closed. Already, however, some houses, led by the recent rise of commerce, had boldly appeared on the hills, not daring to go as far as the seashore.

One after another, they laid down the hypotenuse of a mild, orderly boldness. Close to it, the appeal of trade, with its centrifugal pull, had strewn some isolated small buildings along the length of the shore, following the same line as the plane trees and the willows. In front of them, three or four caïques swayed in the water.

I could not see the marshland, since then the Maremma . . .

Such thoughts preoccupied me in the morning, Louisa, as I descended the steps on Patreos Street to go to the printing office. The city and I had grown up together. Neither one of us could deny the light or the darkness of the other—the light and darkness of a lifelong daily acquaintance. These steps, for example, that join the upper and the lower parts of town, were built exactly seven years ago and embellished by lampposts with gas lights and by beautiful handrails, all made in England. I looked at them again and, it seems, I was in the way, for, this being Christmas Eve, many children were in a hurry to go down these steps to the shops located on the main commercial streets. I was certain that up to now they had never noticed the fixed picture within which they came tumbling down, holding the hand of a young governess: the wide marble steps, the buildings with the overhangs, and, at the end of the street, the mountains across the way, seemingly resting on the sea. I do not know if there exists a place without its time; the children did well to ignore the anguish of both.

A butcher was bringing up slaughtered turkeys and pigs, his

long apron stained with blood. A group of men with dark suits, canes, and top hats were walking in his path. They were forced to stop their conversation and make room for him, so he wouldn't interrupt the straight line of his ascent. In fact, they turned their heads as soon as the butcher had moved on to observe, quite surprised, the tangle of man and animal, dead naked flesh and bloody cloth, celebration and commercial sacrifice, as if they did not know where it belonged. As the men passed by me, merrily conversing about their card game of the day before, I squeezed the wrapped package I was carrying to the printing shop. The dead animal, the blood, and the sacrifice, I dare say, were not visible through the packing paper that protected the books and my publications. Once again I felt a pain in my heart and held on to the handrail. It was very cold, but I did not let go of it until I had descended all the steps.

Panayiotis Eumorphopoulos's printing shop, the Phoenix, was at the lower end of Patreos Street, near the waterfront. They always welcomed me warmly. Something like kinship had grown between Panayiotis and me since the time when, years ago, I was summoned to bid farewell to his brother at Ayia Paraskevi, here in Patras. One might say that he died under favorable circumstances. One of the last living heroes of the Revolution, he had lived in relative isolation on his farmland. In keeping with the ideas of the Revolution, he had taken part in subsequent revolutionary movements. The title of major general had been awarded to him very late. He breathed his last a few days after the celebration for the fiftieth anniversary of the outbreak of the Revolution, at which he had presided and had delivered the oration. I had heard him, and I admired him.

So I entered the printing shop. The speech I had given that resulted in my fleeing to Italy to escape Othon's gendarmerie had been printed here at the Phoenix. If I am not mistaken, the Achaian Youth had provided the funds for the publication. My first theatrical work had been printed here also, as well as the famous speech I gave in the elections of '72—when Asimakis had arrived after dark with a large crowd and called on me to give a speech. Louisa, I cannot stop thinking about him. This morning, as I was entering the printing shop, I was practically overcome with tears.

One more reason why I do not like a floor with black and white tiles, in addition to its apparent but inescapable similarity to a chessboard: it has not been long since Asimakis was here and we were all talking together—the word "all" was still meaningful then—about politics, about art, and about the latest news. Every movement—one of us shifting a chair, another raising a piece of type up to the gas flame to see it better, a third clearing the table by picking up the cups and the scattered papers—every movement, I say, got trapped in the symbolism of the floor. Sometimes even our words seemed to be standing or moving around on the tiles. This annoyed me especially, the pawns of words, words that I wanted to be free. I certainly knew that I wanted a utopia; recently, however, I got distressed when things forced me to reflect upon my stalemate.

I leaned on the cabinet where they kept the cases of type and waited for Panayiotis to finish tying the metal type of a page with string. They wouldn't hear of me doing any work around here. I amused myself with the thought that each page has to tie its soul in steel fetters before it allows it to fly in order to put its immortality to the test, the immortality of a few ideas, the only type of immortality I accept, I was thinking, as I heard Panayiotis calling the owner of the coffee shop and ordering the immortal sweet brew: two cups, and don't be late; the rest, later. We were waiting for his sons, who more or less ran the business, but they had gone out to the banks. We were also waiting for Vasilis.

I threw a glance at the backyard through the hazy window. The shade of the roof tiles made a curly line and divided the white wall across the yard in two screens, the bottom one darker and the upper brighter. December sun, low lying. Some wooden packing cases with loose planks were covered with burlap to protect them from the frost. Their contents were not visible. Yes, Panayiotis had grown very old, but he insisted on setting the type himself for the edition of my works.

I approached and placed on the table the package that I had brought with me and had left on the floor. Books, offprints, one-page items, these would defend the immortality of my ideas; but nothing could convince me that they would not be forgotten, all of them, the day after. Vasilis, who wanted to look after the work and would be coming soon, hoped that this time the publication could be funded by the municipality and the citizens. Earlier the same attempt had been unsuccessful. Could it be that it had a premonition of my plans?

Panayiotis took the package. I saw the love in his hands as he opened and folded the packing paper, rolled up the loose string, and finally touched the contents of the package. Carefully, he took the handwritten page, which I had placed at the top. He knew Italian well, but his eyesight was weak. He raised the page toward the light, adjusted his glasses, and read, one syllable at a time:

> *Ricordati di me* . . . .
> . . . . *maremma mi disfece.*
> —Dante

He squinted and read it again. Then he looked at me as if he had lost his king in the word game. Perhaps he noticed compassion for the defeated king in my glance also. He stopped looking at me, read the words again, as if drawn to them by a magnet, and said quietly: "With red ink. And on a plain background."

He did not add anything else. Just the vocabulary of work, which, at this time of day, was elevated to the level of verse.

Vasilis came in the printing shop quite animated owing to the crispness of the December air and to his own visions, which demanded ceaseless vigilance. He was a handsome man. The light recast his already handsome features in the sky blue, the rose, and the gold of the late Renaissance. To be sure, I did not agree with his latest inclination toward French anarchism, a tide that, on the one hand, I respected, but that did not move me. I was older too, much older. I loved him, however, unselfish, theoretical, and combative as he was, the way I knew him years ago—the only one of my close friends who was still living.

He found us counting the pages of my works. I examined them again, as Panayiotis suggested fonts and paper. Every one of them a piece of me, dead. How many times had I given myself up to the small deaths of writing? Voluntarily, I believe, so every one of my works was a symbolic suicide and, at the same time, a probable victory in that always noble duel.

He reminded me that both of us had been invited by a mutual acquaintance for Christmas dinner the following day, and he asked me if I would be going. I would go after all, so to be with people and to stop circling around a certain adverb. Our acquaintance's invitation, however, did not stop annoying me somewhat. He had also studied in Italy, and we had the same ideas, more or less. He took care not to make them known, so his inherited wealth was becoming more and more deeply rooted in their successful obliteration. But I hasten to add that periodically he had contributed financially to our activities, and we were indebted to him.

The light in the yard was now bright enough. Vasilis approached the window, opened the book that he had taken from the table, and began to read a passage from my first theatrical work, *John Milton*. Milton's words were heard one at a time:

> *Why, oh, Cromwell, does the work of our hands get destroyed so quickly? Tell me, you who can already see the future from the skies. . . . How many times do you appear in the darkness that surrounds me, radiant, like the times when you returned from the war for freedom? . . . So do you exist, or is immortality a*

vain consolation for unfortunate human beings, perhaps? . . . The stars are inclined toward a brighter center; humanity is inclined toward freedom. Yes, only the works of tyranny and barbarity pass on irretrievably; the works of truth, of freedom, disappear only momentarily, and brighter they. . . .

He threw a glance at me before continuing.

As soon as he began to read, I sat down in the nearest chair. While listening to him carefully, I began to find the beauty on the face of the reader vain—or thus it seemed to me—and, more important, the beauty of my work vain as well. However, was the beautiful in each instance implicated in its own cancellation? What did the end of romanticism mean for my work? A useless arsenal of rhetoric? I was not sure about anything.

I was only sure that I liked Vasilis's morning reading; despite my melancholic disposition, I was fortunate on this day to hear in the voice of a good friend a passage of my work. No, I could not stand outside of either him or my work—or, furthermore, of the significance everything assumed in the printing shop that morning.

The municipal band stood outside the printing shop. We invited the musicians to come in, and we welcomed them with the usual greetings. They were standing, forming a semicircle of dark blue pants, red jackets, and gold-braided hats. The trumpets and the trombones stood up to play Christmas carols. They dragged the light from the entrance in their orbit, rounding it like a bright star. The beats of the bass drum quickly transformed the printing shop into a cavelike sound box.

The vibration of my heart led me to other Christmases, Louisa. We had returned from Ithaca and were living in those ruins around the fortress. Some men with *foustaneles* and musical instruments had come to sing Christmas carols; if I remember correctly, they had drums and clarinets. For the first time I bonded with whatever I saw, whatever I touched, whatever was happening around me. Years later, I left to go abroad, I lived in

Athens, but here I returned, to this laboratory of color and light, to check my experience against the simple line of the horizon. Only thus could I appropriate the alien. The city and the rejoicing nature around it offered me hours of self-knowledge; tonight I shall not call them gifts of the Danaans.

The musicians stopped playing. A boy wearing a similar uniform, his hair cut straight across the top, with eyes that seemed amused by the role they played, passed his hat around. We put in our contributions. Panayiotis brought a bottle of wine. He passed out glasses, with the good humor of a king who scatters coins on the streets after his crowning to keep the evil spirits away from the outcome of whatever game. We exchanged greetings once again for Christmas and for a happy new year; also wishes that the end of our century, which was swiftly approaching, be blameless, peaceful, and sinless. I reminded them that the new year was above all the one hundredth anniversary of the French Revolution. Raising my glass, I proposed that we drink to its accomplishments and to its endlessness—and that the next century be better yet.

I drank the wine in a single gulp without thinking of my heart condition. I must say that I was not optimistic about the twentieth century, even though optimism (which is a necessary quality of a public speaker) had formerly been my second nature more or less. The next century interested me very little; I can say that it even frightened me. I had melted my metal in the mold of my own century. I could not refer to myself except retrospectively. For me, in the eyes of the world, the poet, the orator, the revolutionary, the dramatist, and the deputy—let the one in love dwell always in the shadow—for me, then, the twentieth century was simply a wishful inclination: useful, on the one hand, for the prophet, but at the same time rendered useless by the need for blessings.

Again I beg you, Louisa, to be indulgent of the flashbacks on these pages, for so many things are gathering and seeking to be brought to light that the order is sometimes lost. Twenty years have gone by—it was in February, I think—since the army doctors called me to speak at the memorial of a fellow doctor, Ioannis Vasiliou, a volunteer, who had been killed in the Battle of Crete. I remember well the cold and the crowd in the cathedral in Athens. In finishing, I had said that we were at the beginning of the end of all great works of the nineteenth century—specifically, that "*our century is reaching its end; it is approaching its denouement.*" Even then I believed in a better outcome, as, for that matter, was the hope of its most brave youthful hours. Tonight I could add that, if it is reaching its end, if it is approaching its denouement, this denouement at certain points seems to contradict the logic of its original formulation.

The municipal band had left. It was playing Anglo-Saxon Christmas carols in the business district—joyful notes for a future when oratory will be left out of the accoutrements of politicians and of those in love and, as a result, their souls will be restrained.

I stepped outside the door of the printing shop also. It was cold, and I went back inside. The time was passing. Panayiotis and Vasilis continued talking about the publication. Then Vasilis left, reminding me one more time about the invitation on the morrow. Did I perhaps want to leave with him? I answered that I preferred to walk back alone.

I wanted something else also. When we were left alone, I took Panayiotis's hand and kissed it. I left right away.

I left agitated. My heart beat so hard that I had to stop. I saw the familiar picture: the mauve curtain of bare mountains, perpendicular to the dark blue sea, closed off the straight line of the street. Its folds, in sharp relief against the glaze of winter, did not keep any secrets from me—and my mind wandered to mutual confessions of bygone days.

I proceeded to the square in the center of town, the one known as Néa Ekklesía tou Démou, so called because years ago the country's first constitution was read here, near an old spring. That constitution was also the result of a revolt. Today the city was showing me the dead among the living. Its final gift perhaps? I do not know; but, passing by the square, I thought of Kalamogdartis reading, one word at a time, "a military man, good looking." Later on, having been plagued by imprisonments and wars, he surrendered to the tranquillity of a bribed death. I did not envy him only for these things but also for his signature—Erimitis tou Halkomata—and a country place where he often stayed to translate, among other things, Dante's *Inferno*. The square had taken his name, but soon it was relieved of his allusions to the constitution by taking the names of kings.

How many times did I give speeches here!

Outside the building of the Apollo Theater, a man with a top hat and a woman wearing a hat, dark jacket, and golden yellow skirt had approached the box office. Nearby someone else wearing a *foustanela,* vest, and fez was standing in front of the geometric wrought-iron shapes of one of the gates. My eyes also caught sight of two Catholic priests with wide-brimmed hats walking on the street and did not fail to take notice of the statues on the roof of the theater and the five arches of the balcony exactly above the five arches of the entrance, before withdrawing from the lustrous facade with gloomy thoughts. All of this past year only operettas have been heard at the Apollo Theater: perhaps that, too, had contributed to my melancholy.

You are aware, Louisa, of my faith in Italian melodrama. Since the time I was studying in Italy, I have worshiped it for its seriousness and its patriotism. It would have been enough for me to have written only the verses of a popular aria instead of my two dramatic works. In the spring of this past year, La Salle's French troupe arrived from Ermoupolis by way of Athens—to put us to sleep, as my father would say in times past, with the jests of Lecocq and others. However, ten years ago, in order to include one of Lecocq's modernistic operettas in its program, a theater company presented it as a comic melodrama, translating even its libretto into Italian. In fact, it put the ones in charge to sleep, thus managing to get into the theater on the sly, and the audiences in the end accepted what had happened. But this year, with six operettas in succession, and with the crowds happily flowing to attend them and coming out of the theater as if in a torpor, I felt that my personal history was gravely wounded. Even if you maintain, Louisa, that a history is never exhausted in only one person, and you certainly would be correct, is such public degradation suddenly possible?

In order to avoid the theater but also the patrons of the cafés in the arcades around Georgiou Square, I crossed the square quickly. I could not help noticing the trash that was gathered in the empty basins of the two French fountains. The speech of the water flowing through the mouth of the bronze lions had been stopped. The flute at the lips of the naked man at the top of the upper fountain had lost the scale of the mythical forest, while Eros, misbehaving and childish at the man's feet, had also forgotten the whistling of the arrow. The orange trees around the perimeter of the square had been uprooted in view of the prospect of an ambitious tree-planting project, which for the time being had not taken place. In the summer, at least, an outdoor orchestra played in the square till late. In the dead of winter, everything had become chilled to the bone.

It was not only because of the cold—when a spark from the glance of a woman could always nullify it. It seems that not many days have gone by since I saw you for the first time. One afternoon I was standing in the square and talking with friends.

You crossed the square—but with great hesitation. You looked at me, and I, who until then had not been aware of your feelings, saw your eyes wide open and understood.

It did not take me long to arrive at the house that my father had left me. Two or three rooms were still mine. These constituted the only possessions of a descendant of two generations of well-to-do merchants who had consciously wasted his property. As a local newspaper wrote lately on the occasion of my brother's death, "a family distinguished in the past for its wealth and power." Did you hear, by the way, that he died? The two of us had been virtual strangers for a whole lifetime.

The house was built when we came back from Ithaca. Of the old families, those that had been distinguished because of their wealth and power, none had to buy land in the newly erected lower town. By right each family was given land to build on, which was chosen by lot. Because the upper part of town was declared national property, the landowners were compensated with (among other things) property in the lower part of town. It was in their interest, naturally, since Kapodistrias had assigned his friend from Corfu, the engineer Stamatios Voulgaris, to draw up plans for the new city. He laid it out on the marshland between the hill that held up the old city and the sea that held the future of the new one. Basing his vision in history, Voulgaris placed the city exactly where Roman engineers had built the capital of a formerly robust Achaian confederation. Roman emperors favored the city because of its location and beauty—favors that sometimes were returned. For example, when Antinous died, the people of Patras responded to Hadrian's love for their city and showed respect for his loss by erecting two statues of the emperor's friend.

I am writing the above to you, Louisa, because this city's connection with Italy has given me great pleasure all along (you know very well what Italy means to me), but also because I feel the friendliness of a past at the threshold of an unknown new century. I return to my subject in order to close it by writing to you that the governor's modesty did not allow him to accept Voulgaris's suggestion that the city be called Ioannoupolis. Patras kept the name of its mythical founder Patreus for the consolation of continuity.

Once you had asked me why I liked Kapodistrias, suspecting perhaps that there were other reasons besides my stand against the monarchy. I had answered that there were not many subjects about which I had an opinion different than his, ending the conversation right there. I do not know what had prevented me from relating to you the following incident. You might as well hear it now. I had difficulty memorizing a short speech in the archaic language, a language that (I hope) I never spoke or wrote, as I was seeking in this area also a short breath of freedom. The teacher had me walk the fixed number of steps, bow, and recite many times; as a matter of fact, the last time he had me wear the national costume, so I would not feel as if I were masquerading. Still, I shivered when I, a young student, stood in front of the governor's dark frock coat and addressed him as a passerby of Patras. He was then preparing a national assembly and was going around the country with three generals of the Revolution. All of them appeared in front of me in the flesh, although, up to that time, they had been something like dragon-slaying saints. People placed palms everywhere to welcome their savior, something that did not prevent the powerful of the countryside from laying down their own plans. The governor seemed moved as he observed the students of one of the first schools of the country lined up in front of a wall of local chieftains over which sparkled silver-coated arms; soon it would be shown that it was not the silver but the spark of conspiracy that made the glorious weapons shine. The governor raised his glance from the lined-up children to the lined-up arms, and there it lingered, gloomy—unless, Louisa, I am allowing hindsight to intervene as I interpret the scene.

I quickly found my courage. My initiation into oratory took place during this short address. At that moment something else happened as well. The governor bent down and stroked my hair.

As a teenager I used to think that the white hand came and rested on my hair every time the combination of vineyards, sea, and red slanted sun demanded a white spot as a type of optical relief—to tone down my emotional involvement in the transparency of color; to remind me that inevitably I was the destined one; and also to remind me of the whiteness of Hades, since, two years after his visit to Patras, the governor was assassinated.

We had moved into the house, with which you are familiar because of your nighttime visits, when something like madness hit everyone after Kapodistrias's assassination, and they all threw themselves into the two-year civil war. That is when we began losing our property—but there was enough left to support my studies in Athens and later in Pisa.

You noticed my household, which was being reduced to fewer and fewer items. Why should I be ashamed? Day by day I was becoming poorer—and this is exactly what public opinion does not forgive in someone who was formerly well-to-do—with my consent, however. The situation did not seem to bother you, except for the times we parted ways: they were not just a few. If my memory does not fail me, early on you had said that even if I were so lucky as to see my dreams come true, it would not be enough to justify the denial of a more normal life. Painfully, your observations can be heard tonight also, Louisa, but I have no regrets. At some point you stopped discussing the subject, probably realizing that if I could devote myself to the risky pleasure of ideas, then I could also fall totally in love with you—even though many of our secret meetings were mere glass fragments.

These rooms, then—unworthy of the ancestral prestige but worthy of the lonesome man writing to you—are near Kapodistrias Square. Your secret visits had required that you remember the location. It had been called the Marcato because the first marketplace of the lower town was located here, and the streets that connected it to the waterfront were the first to be built. Many of your fellow islanders, who had come from the Ionian Islands to join the surviving merchants, settled here. It was they who first used the name Marcato, as a reminder of their own lively marketplaces and as a wish for the same vigor here; also, in order that the operation of an older marketplace in the same location at the time of the second Venetian occupation would not be forgotten. As was the case with almost all the houses in town, our house had a balcony over the arches of an arcade of shops. The fifth arch was a little wider and thus allowed the entrance of a carriage through a smaller arcade that traversed the building and led from the main street in front to an alley of shacks in the back. The entrance to the house was on the side, through the small arcade, so the front of the building was left to the shops. Across the street from our house was the entrance to another house, identical to ours. The two facades, in unison with each other and with the other similar residences on the street, formed a curtain in front of the shacks that were crammed around a multistoried brick factory of that period. You used to come from the back alleys so no one in front would spot you.

The others came from the main street. It seems that I can hear them again—voices of a crowd that had walked on foot one cold evening from the center of Patras and ended up at my house. In their hands they carried candles. Asimakis was in front. I went out on the balcony to thank the night demonstrators, who had formed a new organization to support my candidacy in the elections. I responded to their persistence that I speak and went down to the street. We walked to Kapodistrias Square nearby. I got up on a makeshift platform—made out of barrels and boxes. My speech, entitled "Awakening," was printed the following day at the Phoenix printing shop. (Is my morning visit perhaps drawing me toward this memory?)

Halcyon days, nights rather, and words of the kingfisher:

Did you ever consider for what reason a people will grant power . . . ?

The true political man, oh, fellow citizens, should have an extensive and first-rate education, understanding of the nation, knowledge of the essence of all things. . . .

To go deep into the past, to know the present, to be inspired by the spirit of his century and on his forehead to feel the breezes of the future. . . .

Because politics is knowledge and foreknowledge, estimation and inspiration, creation and foresight. In his heart he should hear all the heartbeats of virtue, of charity. . . .

He should be a man not only of light but of self-denial and sacrifice. . . .

The true politician is a mysterious being, although very bright. He is society's magus, discovering the stars of the future. He is a hierophant, he is a prophet. . . .

He appears peculiar toward many and eccentric toward others. . . .

Do not ask questions about his diet, what he eats, when he sleeps; he is always on the lookout. . . .

Do not expect him always in the streets or in the crowded places of enjoyment. Isolation is for him concentration on life, conception of the ideal, outline of a better society. Such a man goes into caves, fasts in Thebaids, walks in the desert, and from there comes, in time, carrying in his hands lights, pearls, manna, and tosses them to the people. And when the hour is struck by his God, then thought becomes energy, the hermit comes into the crowd, mingles with the people, and, pointing the way to a new life, walks with them toward the bright and prosperous city, the one dreamed of in the desert. . . .

Thus I understood my position as a politician, as a poet, and—I insist—as a lover. You stood sometimes in the light and sometimes in the darkness of that strange man who gave speeches about deserts. No hermit was ever able to defeat the idea of Eros; transforming it is something else. Alone, in love in a most radical way, I loved the crowd in the square too, in the same radical way as one who has renounced his class.

The next day, when I came across the name of the square as I was reading the daily press, the hand of the governor touched my hair once again and filled me with melancholy. What meaning did I have for the gathered crowd of the day before? What meaning did the crowd have in the solitude of the day that was to follow for me? Yesterday, they had lit the front of my house with candles. In their light I saw the symmetrical railings of the porch, the pediment of the balcony door, and the blue meander under the roof come alive. Later on in the square, I saw the faces trembling by a different light, recalling other faces, other candles, other situations. If the neoclassical style took me back to a lost symmetry, what is the meaning of the compression of time and of situations in the events of the square?

Certainly I did not ask out loud. I remember, however, that when I stopped speaking the people were left motionless and quiet as if they were seeing the body of a voice slowly leaving the square. When they lost sight of it, they raised me on their shoulders and carried me triumphantly to my house. Until then, I had been elected representative to the Chamber of Deputies only once and one other time I had been defeated—and I would not be elected deputy in the elections that were to take place in a few days.

Louisa, the more persistent an idea becomes, the more difficult it is for that idea to remain identified with specific individuals. I am thinking whether the fear of death accompanies even the incarnation of ideas. Is this blight grounded in the ideas, in individuals, or, more accurately, in the way the two are intertwined, not only in the exceptional but also in the more commonplace histories? The blight of love is no exception.

As I was writing to you, the lamp enfolded my hands and my words in golden gauze. Around me, the darkness of the winter night had become complete, and I was envious of it for this capability. I turned the knob and increased the flame of the lamp. Brighter now, the light explores certain pages that I did not take to the printing shop this morning and especially certain reasons that did not allow me to entrust them to Vasilis but rather to spread them out on the table tonight. Without doubt, he must have known of the existence of some, but we kept our private thoughts to ourselves. The fanning out of a sentimental word would be quickly checked and replaced by the words of dispassionate politics. We were ashamed of the passions of our souls, even though we were friends.

Nevertheless, no one was ashamed of helping me survive when I did not have even the salary of a deputy and my heart condition prevented me from working. Both you and everyone else were aware of my heart disease. For most, however, my disease was the devotion of my life to dreams. From my point of view, I tried to work as a humble worker to earn a symbolic reward. Early on, and more and more painfully ever since, I became aware of the antithetical relationship between symbolic and real rewards. In order not to give latitude to myself, in order not to look for excuses, I used to reiterate my decision to stay poor and dependent on my friends—if that could lead to something worthwhile. At this moment I am not looking into where it has led, and I hope you remember that I never accepted your offers, thus avoiding giving our situation another dimension than pure passion.

I just thought of it. I should commemorate those devoted friends on the first pages of the planned edition so I can thank them and join their names indissolubly to mine. As for my work itself, it would not be pointless to dedicate it to a future generation. I like this paternal illusion, for we have vanished, most of us childless. Yes, Vasilis is alive, but he is quite a bit younger. I shall think about it some more. I have a few more days in Patras and fewer yet in Athens. Do not ascribe the untidy recording of these thoughts to me. In writing them, I am trying to commit myself.

They were helping me, even though they knew that my time was not spent only in politics. They appreciated my passion for art and, at the same time, the usefulness of art for our goals. They accepted my passion for you without comment, even though it could even turn me against them at some point.

We were the best we could be; for this reason, sometimes miserable.

It is very late. For how many ruthless hours have I been writing to you?

Allow me one more thought. To the extent that a published work does not consume the life of its creator, to the same extent, I say, an unpublished item cannot boast that it interprets all the cracks. In closing, a life should remain—how can I put it?—always cracked, like a landscape. A great part of it does not fit into the ordeal of being committed to writing, thus converting the history of any future moment to prehistory. Consequently, let these pages that I am writing to you be independent of my life, no matter how much they insist on commenting on it, and, finally, on donating it to you. Let the reason that presses me to write this text to you stay in the dark also.

Have compassion, Louisa, for me and for my words.

I have already thrown some papers in the woodstove. I hope to burn them all before I leave for Athens and afterward—did I write this to you already?—for Syros. Being incompatible with the spirit of the next century, it is quite possible that I shall soon be persecuted on the issue of romanticism. Many papers point to my guilt already in the face of a merciless realism. Better that they burn. This is how I used to burn papers formerly, when I was being pursued as a conspirator. It is certain that the new century will turn against us while attempting to create its own different, but equally tragic, code about the same utopias: poetry, revolution, love. Let it rejoice in its youth, for it too might cry in its old age. What can a new generation give that will be altogether better? Let me think about the dedication I was planning to write. I have time.

In these pages, which, without fail, I shall make sure that you receive, I wish to remain incomplete, if not mutilated as well—the marble of a male body in the fields of Greece: antiquity ends forever when one who served utopia comes to his end.

"*The defeat of the evening will be the renowned victory of the following dawn.*" I do not remember when I wrote this. It seems that I must have been very young.

Now I am an old man, a sedate old man. But I am tired of writing.

Louisa, it was impossible for me to sleep. The need to write to you chased away sleep. I avoided looking at the clock and got up to continue.

I summarize: I learned to read and write in Ithaca, I went to school in Patras, and I continued my studies at the newly created University of Athens and later in Pisa. I should add that, despite the epigrammatic description, there was great enthusiasm. All of us, teachers and students, abandoned ourselves to the ideal of a free country and to the literally manual work that it demanded of us. When your family came from Zakynthos—I was going to school then—you were very young, and you probably do not remember the specific climate of the time. The teachers considered the fact that they had to teach the first free citizens of the new nation very significant. To put it differently, due partially to their own wisdom and partially to the heroic spirit of the times, they did not make a clear distinction between the war and the state in their teaching. After the assassination of Kapodistrias, the civil war, and the first years of the regency, it had become obvious even to us, the students, that every war is not consumed in the act of war. There were also the conversations we heard in our homes and the mutterings in the marketplace. It was as if a river that had disappeared from the face of the earth suddenly had gushed out farther away, laboring to go down to the sea.

Which sea, you had asked me once, looking out of the closed windowpanes at the stormy Ionian. Your voice was low, yet it sounded as if it were ordering the elements to stop their fury. Let them not rest. Their quiescence would have seemed more difficult to bear than the vigor of their fury. Soberly I told you that I would never come out of the riverbed—even if it meant risking our lives as in a game of *yiantes:* yours because love did not have power over me; mine because my ideas labored in a rather dead-end riverbed.

I remember that afternoon; I remember its hopeless pleasure. I do not want to be dragged into the shipwreck of such bodies. They were ours, they were foreign. . . .

Despite what I was telling you, your absence would have meant the absence of the most mystical dimension of my life. I, who have been a man of secrets, admit that. Less wise when I used to inhale you, I had not yet exhausted the study of being secretive. There were times, I confess, that I abandoned myself to the sugary-sweet dream of our cohabitation. If you only knew how pliant I was! Afterward I scoffed at my revery. I do not repent either for the one or for the other. It's only that now the river has gone dry, the river that at every turn allowed me to contemplate always the same landscape.

The same face that belonged to you.

And the sea, having walked off and gone far away.

As the son and grandson of Philikoi, I used to say that when I grew up I would render justice wherever it was due. As if that were not enough—and likely it was not, since I was born on a fateful day—I wanted to get educated. Business did not interest me. I objected to my father's insinuations, even though I never objected to the necessity of honest trade, to the modernization of my country, or to the liberal ideas that often traveled along with the products. Father put my brother in charge of his already declining business ventures. He himself, after independence, was the presiding officer of the court of Patras, appraiser of the national lands, and customs inspector. As a result, he neglected looking after his property. Impressed by my performance as a student and by the praises of my teachers, he finally determined that I should study law.

Deep down he was pushing me toward politics. Every family of titled landowners aspired to have a politician in its midst as compensation for the money contributed, the blood shed, and the destruction suffered for the sake of the nation, many times as compensation for nothing. He would be obliged not only to restore but to increase what had been. Otherwise, the family would be in danger, since the equilibrium of life had changed. My refusal to follow the prevailing perception of the political man certainly must have harmed, in its turn, our family interests. But I could not imagine myself much different from the person that I was. Louisa, you might as well know this also: that I distanced myself from my patrimony by deed in order to devote myself to dreams. If the subject comes up, I shall write to you more on this.

You had your father's and your husband's estate—both quite large. You were sustained by the security that very expensive Belgian lace gives a woman. I do not argue, you dared to rebel by having an illicit love affair. You tasted a bite of the forbidden apple, but knowledge demands the sum of its mistakes. Or am

I especially harsh? Certainly I do not blame you; you were one of the most courageous women of your time. Your courage could not but cost you more than any lace. Nor did it give you any sense of security. I remember tears.

As for myself, yes, I was a citizen of the world—I mean to say, a subject of contemplation and inspiration who ignored boundaries—and I did not have many contemporary native role models. I liked to see for myself in faraway lands the same anguish of life. The lack of money many times cut short even the most inexpensive dreams, but I had assumed that this would happen in the life I chose. Who knows, some dreams need to be canceled in any case. However, your objections to exposing your own financial well-being, I have to tell you finally, detracted from you somewhat in my thoughts. I tell you again, knowledge demands the sum of its mistakes in almost the same way as life demands its death. This was one of the sore points, unmentionable and common in all relationships, that I stepped on in order to turn against you when you left one time, blaming me, rather equating my dreams with my poverty. You were also cruel with me: the counterpoint, I would say, of a mutual tenderness.

I studied the Greeks and the Romans for the beauty of their texts and for the purpose of defending a future that steered its course according to the stars of a distant past. I read intensely the socialist writings of my day, as well as European literature. I tried to avoid the danger of pedantry, which is the same in some ways as the danger of provincialism, and to abandon myself in the sea of another type of dangerous sailing.

I used to write poems while still a child. My father said that I had taken after my mother's Ionian heritage, which later on I would have to subject to the logic of legal expression. When I finished school in Patras, I excelled in the exams by composing an oration following all the rules of rhetoric.

All these years Patras grew larger. The landscape changed little: some vineyards were uprooted and some marshes were dried up in order to build the new city. To be sure, great tracts of vineyards and swamps still remained. While a teenager, I happened to be walking in the marshes. A green sheet hid the victims of malaria. Were they the round eyes of birds or motionless souls that scrutinized me from the nearby rushes and reeds? Suddenly they flew away to hide elsewhere. I did not forgive the marshes for taking away Grandma and my dear mother, whom the fever had greatly tormented as if she were responsible for the duel between the uninhabited and the inhabited, between stagnant death and the comfort of future homes.

I learned that nature takes revenge—but blindly, I thought, blindly. I used to look for my mother at every one of the first homes in the new city. However, just as a child grows up and learns not to cry in front of people, at some point I got used to her death, thus in part releasing the place from wrongdoing. I did not write even one verse for Mother. Only two or three lines when I was in my twenties, when one still believes that life goes on paper without a mask; and I confess that now and then it manages to do so. Perhaps part of my sadness was channeled into the funeral orations when I spoke of revolutionaries and heroes as the most affectionate losers. I often believed that I was preparing to write a long poem for her. I was not able to write it. I continuously postponed its composition while the green landscape withdrew before the hues of the city: terra-cotta for the roof tiles, white marble for the porticos and the balconies, ochre or indigo or red for the plaster, black for the metal parapets.

Fate relied mostly on my birth at sea to give destination to my life, without even untying the blindfold around her eyes. There were times when I fought against blind destiny, I, a descendant of the Enlightenment. There were other times, most of them actually, when I was enthused by its pure light, I, a most devoted romanticist. Sometimes I have the feeling, Louisa, that we romanticists never had a specific country, all of us having been born on the ship of refugees. Fallen from the innocence of paradise, forced to deal with wandering, with the internalization of exile, and, even more so, with nostalgia for an ideal country.

I mean to say that I longed for Greece even while I was living in Greece. It is strange, but I thought of her with the longing I felt for her when I was studying in Italy. It is even stranger that the same—but to a lesser degree—happened with regard to Italy. All the time I was living there, in some way I missed people gone by. It is understandable: these were troubled times for Italy also, full of danger and oaths.

You did not appear surprised that Italy, both the idea and the reality of Italy, held on to half of my feelings. From the time I was very young, I spoke and wrote Italian, the second language of Patras, as well as of the neighboring Ionian state. Certainly I felt close to other places as well—not because I found myself there at some specific moment but because at exactly that moment it happened that the places were hanging in midair between two countenances, two moments. This moved me. Venturing once again to simplify things to the point of being simplistic, I am thinking, Louisa, that, perhaps, for free people there is no other country than Hades—not for the unbiased justice one can find there, if what people say is true, but for the ammunition that every once in a while it grants to the living. For what other reason was *The Divine Comedy* a guiding text at the time of the Risorgimento in Italy?

A little while ago I destroyed the draft of a letter I had written from Pisa to the Typaldos brothers in Patras. For a period of time they had taken refuge in Patras because of problems they were having on their island (Cephalonia) with the English. I had visited them in Italy. They had been helpful to me by introducing me to Montanelli, professor of law and courageous liberal leader.

Looking quickly at the draft (I wonder whether the Typaldos brothers have kept my letter), I remembered the room I had as a student—the divan, the light of the lamp, the view toward Santa Maria Street, the Arno River crossing the melancholic city. In fact, I referred to the river—in words reminiscent of those days—as *"one of Napoleon's armies in the deserts of Africa."* The following day was All Saints' Day, a time when the living visit the souls of the dead. The mention of this day guided my pen to a succession of thoughts that led to the East: to the beloved, I would say, of an old God. . . .

.Everything was harmoniously tied together in the map of sentiments and written in the small neat letters of a twenty-one-year-old young man. There were also hints of my participation in the Philological Society of Pisa. Eight years before we met, one of the Typaldos brothers was one of its founding members. The ideas of the society at the time I was writing to them had bloomed in the verses of the most important poets of the Ionian Islands.

To my father I wrote often. I did not avoid rereading some excerpts before destroying the letters. I imagine you know how hesitantly we throw our life in the fire. For your sake, I saved part of the magic from the pyre: not to forget to send my tuition; while teaching in the Sapienza Building the professors wear gowns and elsewhere black clothes; they introduced the subject in Latin and developed it in Italian, as a matter of fact, in the Tuscan dialect; we had school breaks on the feast days of saints, the last six days of Mardi Gras, the day of the dead, the name day of the ruling monarch—mainly on these days; we

Orthodox went to church in Livorno, where there was also the cemetery of the large Greek community—with which, Louisa, my family had old commercial ties.

To my father's question pertaining to with whom I kept company, I had answered that I associated primarily with students from the Heptanesa, since they constituted the largest number of Greeks studying in Italian universities and for other reasons. I wrote to him about the proceedings at the consulate that were never ending, even for the most trivial matter; about the physical examinations in Ancona upon our arrival from Greece; about the obligatory visit to the consul and to the prominent Greeks of Livorno; and about the famous Café di Commercio as well. As for the trip from Ancona to Pisa, I wrote to him that I traveled by coach and that it was fascinating. Most of us students lived in the old buildings in the center of town, the buildings with the blackened walls, the dark entrances, the narrow staircases. Somewhere I was asking him to go to the trouble of sending me more woolen clothes as well as money to buy new gloves and some more clothes of the style worn in Italy at that time, unless he was giving me permission to borrow an amount of money from our acquaintances in the Greek community. Somewhere else I was asking if he had received the orders I had sent him by a third party. In one of the last letters, I informed him that we were all excited about the brilliant performances of melodramatic works taking place that winter in the theater in Pisa.

He had responded that I should look after my duties and nothing else. The theater was fine, but it was expensive and dangerous, even though I was nearing the end of my stay in Italy. In previous letters he had written that he was well but was quickly getting old—an event that he considered unimportant in comparison to my expected "crown" from the Italian university. It was not necessary that I go to Patras—better that I stay there to study and, if possible, to finish more quickly. He had sent me a basket full of woolen clothes and dried foods, he wrote, and I should go to Livorno to get it. Beware of everyone and of everything, he wrote—I should be able to understand what he wanted to say: uphold the dignity of my upbringing, the pride for my country, and the good reputation of my family.

He often wrote to me news from Patras. Such and such a businessman, a relative of ours, had died at a ripe old age, leaving a ripe old fortune. The situation was always unstable. Copies of the newspaper *Kartería* were confiscated two times, and the takeovers of the vineyards filled the city with angry villagers asking for explanations and, along with the rest of the people, a constitution. The government leaders were concerned. The constitutional revolt in Athens, he wrote later on, was celebrated enthusiastically in the central square and on the streets of the city. He wondered whether the people would be able to rely on the constitution now. In another letter he informed me that one of my fellow students in Athens, a close friend of mine, after practicing law for a short time had decided to become a public prosecutor. He had already become engaged to the daughter of a wealthy landowner from Zakynthos who had become established in Patras many years ago. Their wedding was to take place soon. The bride was well-to-do and beautiful, according to what people said. He wished that I have the same good fortune, with his blessing.

I was informed about your existence by this letter of my father's. I do not need to write you that I had no objection to beautiful women, but their wealth did not interest me. My friend, nevertheless, was lucky: the property of the bride would somehow support the career of a talented and aspiring husband. In what way did he differ, this educated man, this man inspired by beautiful ideas—how was he different, Louisa, from my father and my grandfather on the subject of marriage? He was inferior, since he had the good fortune of living in an age when he did not have to deal with major dangers. Certainly that age had its own dangers—as long as one wished to struggle. However, it was not the same. After he decided to become a public prosecutor, it was to be expected that he forget his liberal self, the self that I had become fond of in our all-nighters during our student days in Athens. Was I just, or was I envious of the certainty of a career and a wedding, against which I was to turn very soon, as I was making at that time—or, rather, confirming—the basic choices of my life?

For this reason, you belonged in my choices also, long before I saw you and was overtaken by you. You would continue to belong to them forever, in spite of the rebellions or silences on both sides every once in a while—in spite of the clashes. Love quickly forgets: merely a cricket in a coastal olive grove. How many people in love have not fished compassion for themselves out of the salty blue water?

I shall not continue. Would that I had the opportunity once again to hear your arguments against my choices, when you said—rather correctly—that I had entrapped you. Your voice would be painful to me. This time I, the unbelieving young man, would not interrupt you to project the superiority of my own knowledge, my training in logic, my scorn for all the worldly things you represented, the belief that ideas surpass even the ability of crystal not to crack. I learned my lesson; ideas also crack following the crooked line of love, and they return now, at the dawn of Christmas Day, asking for the uncracked crystal. To put it a little differently, whatever I had taken away from you comes back now and asks for its old share—along with the interest.

The savings of a piggy bank, you had said once, referring to my finances. I shall not indulge myself by saying that it was full of gold coins—nothing of the kind, with the present currency. Count, however, with the generosity of pleasure; with the need for tenderness; with the jasmine in your hair; with the imperishability of naked bodies; with the daring of the forbidden; with the cost of separations; with fingers intertwined, both of us thinking that the death of lovers is the most cruel, the death of a hermit the most imperceptible, that the two of us. . . .

You can tell that I cannot continue.

I call it unbelievable. Hearing about you from my father, I was not frightened by the omen of our future as it was formulated in his last sentence. I limited myself to denouncing the fiancé, since I would win later, by some means, and with my father's blessing, the same woman.

As all these things glide on the arch of the question mark tonight, I ask myself, on the one hand, whether the grafting of your existence onto mine could have taken place apart from the years I spent in Italy—when I was deciding, as I already wrote to you, on the components of my life. On the other hand, I ask myself if my love for you was not based on something even much older than my father's letter. What was and what was not accidental is not always significant. In the sacred malaise of love, what is accidental has its own strict determinism so as to return to something very old and forgotten, so as to be bound with it in the most heterogeneous agronomy. Once—who knows how?—I must have seen you, garden fresh and protected from the wind, taking root on my branches, spreading forth your earthly colors iridescently: branches of the forest that chose mysterious myths and mountain landscapes; beasts of the shadows and rays of light; the company and the silence of other trees; the sound of an ax that is approaching.

You blossomed in the most forbidden union, giving the spirituality of an experiment to our love. Does it matter if it did not succeed?

Louisa, as I write these things to you, I do not know if I can be called the archetype of the forest—even though it gained in proportion because of your iridescence—I, who was born on the sea. It appears that, until my final hour, I shall not be able to avoid mistakes, since love has a need for metonymy (if not for an actual mistake). For this reason forgive this attempt at poetry one more time—a poetry without style, perhaps mistaken, on the brink of dying, but coming from the heart.

Shortly before Christmas 1843, my name was entered in the register of graduates of the University of Pisa with the following note: "Patrasso, Giurisprudenza." I wrote to my father right away to inform him of the event, as well as of the fact that I would not be returning right away. I still had some business to finish. It had to do with the large demonstration we were preparing in the theater of Pisa, but I did not mention it to him, since our letters were being censored.

For the same reason, I had never written to him about the suspicions of the Italian police, the illegal publications, the searches of student residences, the arrests, the trials, the deportations, the fact that some of us were forbidden to appear in the theater and in well-known cafés. Besides, he knew about these things from other sources. Nor did I write to him about the famous printing shops—bookstores, which were often visited by commissaries who sensed in these places the activities of those Greek students who belonged to the patriotic society known as La Giovine Italia (Young Italy). Nor about the Stamperia di Eugenio Pozzolini in Livorno, where my own ode was printed. I did not refer to our banquets on the anniversary of the War of Independence, which fatefully coincided with my birthday. One banquet in particular occupied the police of the duchy of Tuscany for several months. They accused us Greeks—as if it were not enough that we put laurel stems in our boutonnieres—of accompanying the orchestra by singing patriotic tunes, of raising our glasses to ambiguous toasts, and of causing damage to the chandelier of the place.

The accusations were true—except for the fact that the account referring to the extent and the truth of the events was printed in a proclamation in Livorno, and the reference to this city was considered by many to be misleading. From the list of names that accompanied the cheers and the wishes and the slogans for extermination, it became apparent that the banquet guests, most of them from the Ionian Islands, cursed the English governor and swore in the name of well-known patriots. From the fact that we all ran to embrace the Greek flag, shouting cheers for our country, for freedom, and for the king while the orchestra played "What Are You Waiting For, Friends and Brothers?" one thing became apparent, Louisa: which wind was blowing at the time that swept me for life in its whims. I owe it to you, however, to explain that, being one of two students from Athens, I did not equate freedom and country with the king, as the students from the Heptanesa often did. Since those early days, I was against Othon, the king, and I never cheered for him.

Furthermore, I was lucky to have connections with the most liberal intellectuals of Italy, intellectuals of such repute as Mayer, Angelica Palli, and Tommaseo. They had rallied around the periodical *Antologia*. As you know, I corresponded with Tommaseo later on, as did quite a few from the Ionian Islands who had met him either in Italy or in Corfu during the five years he was living there in exile. We all were of the opinion then that the problems of Greece, of the Ionian Islands, of Dalmatia, and of Italy were common to all, despite some particularities. I tell you again that I am concerned about the fate of this correspondence, which at one time I had given to you for safekeeping. Would that it still exists! If Vasilis asks for it, I beg of you one more time to entrust it to him.

The theaters were the sheltering forum of a tempestuous time. At some point I must have spoken to you (I wonder how) about the demonstration that turned out to be one of the most significant moments of my life, entering my name in the register of Italian history. I shall speak to you about it again, fearing that perhaps in trying to forget me you have forgotten everything. The game of memory has its defeated king also. In January '44, there was to take place at the theater of Pisa a benefit performance by Teresa Brambilla, a soprano famous throughout Europe. That same day she was celebrating her thirtieth birthday. Three other famous singers, all of whom happened to be her sisters—the family had a long singing tradition—were to be present to celebrate her birthday. Teresa Brambilla was singing at a time when arias were being repeated by shady rebels outside the theater on the streets of the cities. The trampling of hooves, as the police approached on horseback, cut off the melody, and wailing, rather than applause, deigned these daring repeat performances worthy.

I had composed an ode for Teresa Brambilla—I think I mentioned it already. I was inviting the diva to travel to Greece to see how the brave die, how by their own blood they rediscover ancient glory, how they achieve victory, how they are praised, how they win the wreath of glory, as long as they are united. Don't forget, Louisa, that the Italians were then dreaming of freedom and the unification of their country. Professor Sylvestro Centofanti translated my ode into Italian prose. The translation was carefully distributed to comrades and sympathizers who had come to the benefit performance.

Have I ever told you about Sylvestro Centofanti's legendary lecture? It took place around that time. Yes, in a full lecture hall, Centofanti read a manifesto for Italian unification whose fighting spirit was based on the recent example of the Greek Revolution. Finally, he read a text in Greek. Even though applause in the classrooms (from which undercover agents were never absent) had been forbidden by the police, and even though the French custom of escorting someone had also been explicitly forbidden, the following occurred: Just as Centofanti stopped speaking, we broke out in applause, cheers, and tears. Cheering him on, we honored him by accompanying him as he exited from the Sapienza Building. He was so moved that, as he was coming out, he came close to getting killed by a passing coach. We escorted him to the river. Until the boat took him across, we stood at attention, clapping continuously. He, standing up, with his hat off, kept waving a handkerchief in response. His face—with the long sideburns, the distinct lips, and, especially, the dark, tearful look—would not shrink in the distance. An hour seemed to have gone by before Centofanti disappeared in the streets across the river.

During that time, I had invited Teresa Brambilla on a mental journey; the times did not rule out its becoming a reality. Tonight I invite you, Louisa, on a different mental journey— the calendar prohibits it from taking place. Just as I invited the soprano to come in sight of the epic song, I now invoke the loss of epic song so you can see the soul of one of its young advocates.

Escaping from the hastily opened fans and from the absorbency of the velvet, the murmurs of the nearby boxes will reach your ears, the murmurs of red lips: He just received his degree in law as well as in poetry, it seems. His name should not be mentioned aloud either in the theater or in the halls—or outdoors. There he is, standing in the corner, near the stage. He is surrounded by other young men. Very proud of today's events. So he is Greek.

Keep looking at me, Louisa, until, caught in the enchantment of your gaze, I turn to see you and to predict our future. My father's prophetic letter was forgotten in my pocket, and I shall forget myself looking at you who until then had been undepicted. To the prospect of our future, I shall juxtapose the feelings of a moment of triumph, insisting that knowledge is not only a moment of triumph or ruin but a sign of their continuous coexistence—thus insisting on the biblical wisdom.

I confess that back then I did not usually entertain such thoughts. If I happened to read them, I passed by them rather quickly. I had the self-sufficiency of youth. I was thrilled by the joy of making a name for myself and of achieving even a minor degree of glory—a justified but, at the same time, vain joy. I believed in the immortality of even my first written words. This was another indication of youth. I had not yet considered that I had grown up on the island where the irony of weaving was discovered—and youth is not concerned with homecoming.

Not that I did not have even then the impression that I was on swampy ground. But the fact that I was on good terms with learning, my ambition, the feeling of destiny, all of these indicated to me that I could conquer, or at least understand, some things forever—and speak in time about them, since it seemed to me that youth would last forever also.

It does not matter. Youth has the luster of a pardonable self-importance.

So you were there?

I shall entrust to you, Louisa, a final Italian memory, knowing that you still will not have a full picture of my life there. Besides, a life that can be remembered to the letter touches on the truth of a police report.

It happened that one time, along with a group of fellow students, I visited the region of the Italian Maremma, not very far from Livorno. I want to make it clear that I did not belong to the Interpreti di Dante, a secret society with its own signs, rules, and oath of solidarity, or to a later society, connected with the Parisian Saint-Simonites. In some way, however, all of us had taken an oath in the name of Dante. His verses mingled with our words to be an example for our lives. I, a foreigner, made the necessary effort to penetrate the symbols of persons and places in *The Divine Comedy* which were self-evident for the natives. I remember my surprise when suddenly I identified the Maremma of Dante's verses with the picture that I saw around me: an immense marshy area near the sea.

We went around the green stagnant waters in a shallow boat: sandy dunes, reeds, rushes, and birds. The villages near Patras came to my mind, as well as crystal-clear references to the Maremma in *The Divine Comedy*, to the stench, the snakes, the fevers, but, most of all, to the cruel fate of a countess. As he rowed the boat, the boatman recounted her story. I hope to find the time to relate it to you in these pages, where other, real events have precedence. It seems strange, but I do not remember if I have ever spoken to you about the unfortunate countess.

I return to my subject. They had begun some work to drain the marshes for the sake of the health of the people living there and the reputation of the region. Fishermen had been living there since ancient times. In a few years I would learn that they saved Garibaldi and his only companion, but even this fact was not enough to finally release the yellowish green Maremma from its dark past.

If at some time my book, which is to be published, arrives in your hands, Louisa, its epigraph will remind you of all the things I wrote above. Sometimes I have the feeling that, just as in the case of love, death also seeks an early reference to something very old and forgotten and that this search can bypass the duration of a lifetime in order to refer to an event that took place many centuries previously. True or not, it does not matter. In the passing of time, and with the support of art, all things stay and hover around us—anonymous, symbolic, unfading.

25 december 1888
patras

Louisa, I woke up very late. As I was preparing some tea in the kitchen, I thought that I should give you a gift on this children's holiday.

Yesterday I was in town all morning, but I did not remember to buy you a gift. I was desperate. I had to give you something, however, so I took a white sheet of paper and drew a railroad, like the one that lately connects Athens and Patras. Rather unskillfully, I confess, I drew a ribbon tied in a bow around the four railroad cars, as if they were boxes in a row. I found the bottle with the red ink—was it necessity or the narcissism of writing that made me have ink of many colors around?—and I wrote over the cars in a curved line "Chrónia Pollá." At the time I was writing it, I remembered Panayiotis's words about the Dantean verses in the printing shop. I would prefer that he print them in black ink, which he would use for the rest of the work, to avoid any insinuations beyond the words themselves and for another reason: something having to do with the anonymity of print.

I woke you up, as couples who have been together for a long time wake up on holidays. I brought you your gift and kissed you again. You squeezed my hand happily. You did not speak, but I understood the promise to safeguard the childishness of maturity as if it were the most expensive gift. I saw your eyes in the dark foliage of years that had rolled by, and from its center I heard the same trill. Wish that it would never end.

We drank tea, sitting at the big table. Here is where I started writing to you yesterday. How was I to think of you afterward? I was not able to avoid the dramatic tone of adverbs, such as "afterward" and an automatic "why," in spite of the danger of stooping down to the most common and even the most ridiculous questions. Without asking you, my question mark was fused in the lines of your face, the face of a mature woman—with no straight lines. I took your hand. You pulled it away softly and folded it in the other one, thus answering by way of a knot. The glow of the stove dispersed the sparkle of your diamond ring, without untying your tightly folded hands. I got up to warm mine. At some point I had to burn the remaining papers that lay in a disorderly pile on the floor, since I did not have a servant. I had straightened up the table myself in order to set it with what was left of an expensive set of china.

I listened to you talking about different things, as if nothing had happened just a little while ago. You probably did not want to deal with questions; besides, it would not have been right for me to direct questions toward you since I also considered them unanswerable. I returned to the table and sat once again across from you. We smiled, I believe.

The cape with the broad, rounded collar was for me a sign of another age, place, and outlook. I never parted either with my recollection of them or with my Italian cape in very cold weather. These last few days, however, it could not protect me from the frost. At noon, as I was going to the house where I had been invited for dinner, I was cold. The glimmer of the diamond of my dream came to my mind time and again: the absolute hardness of minerals. Perhaps the icicle of the present is partly to blame.

I left these thoughts outside the gate. From there on I would be walking in the house of a respectable man who had invited me to share the warmth of his family on this holiday. Yesterday's doubt about this person had noiselessly distilled to a rather friendly feeling—not only because of my obligation as a guest. That is how it was. Climbing the stairs, I had the impression that I recognized every doubt in the ripples of the marble steps. Knocking the freezing hand of the knocker, I was not able to avoid the familiar question: "What is such a rich house for?" He who buries beautiful ideas in a cellar with select wines cannot get drunk from their visionary nectar. Where, I wondered, would the servant take me after opening the door, to the salon or to the cellar? Oh, I wish I were not so fainthearted, I, a former member of the upper class.

As I was giving my cape to the servant, from the corner of my eye I saw the salon through the glass of the six-paneled door. Someone opened it, and I entered with the air of one who feels at home, as the host was coming forward to meet me. The pale winter light became more distinctly white in the reflections of the snow-white linens, the laces, the powdered sugar of the *kourambiethes,* the shining curvature of the silverware, and the carved marble that framed the fireplace. From there the glow of the fire gave the white color an unsteady rose hue, while the crackling of the wood served as a reminder of the rules of the day: fiddle-faddle for the *kalikantzaroi* and good wishes for the hosts. I expressed my wishes for the day as I savored a cognac. As soon as I warmed up a bit—I should have called for a carriage—I was able to see the green ferns in the flower stands, bouquets of flowers in the vases and on the carpets, the pale faces in the oil paintings, the black wing of the open piano, and, finally, the youthful and frightened Europa riding on the almighty bull and crossing blue waves on the ceiling. From the beginning her look belonged to mature love affairs: so the painter knew the secret of his art, if not of his life as well. As I waited for Vasilis and the others, I thought of you having been led to sensuous azures, Louisa.

They came. In a little while they called us to the dining room.

The ritual of the holiday dinner lasted for some time. We then retired to the parlor to enjoy coffee, liqueur, and tobacco. I sat near Vasilis. I told him that, besides the Dantean epigraph, I wanted to add a few lines to thank my friends. I did not even rule out a dedication of my work to younger generations. However, I asked him for the right to take my time with these two items; as I saw it, if I decided to write them, I would probably mail them from Athens, where I intended to go soon. He ought to allow me—I smiled—to put his name next to the names of those I wished to thank, those who comprised the only family I had as a grown-up, if, of course, I decided to compose the note of thanks. I thought again that the friends whom I would mention had all died except for Vasilis, but I did not allude to that.

Without a word, Vasilis approached the piano. He played (curtly, almost out of tune) one of Verdi's arias, the one he knew moved me since way back. When he finished, he let a moment hang in midair, and then he played the same melody in the proper rhythm, so proper, in fact, that for a long time we did not dare to look each other in the eye.

The host's children, a boy and two girls, rushed upon the piano. Christmas music and songs enlivened the atmosphere, wisely breaking up what had united Vasilis and me. Things were as they should be on holidays. As soon as it started getting dark, the light of the candles and the chandelier quickly covered the blue waves on the ceiling with yellow varnish. They became greenish: I did not avoid thinking of the waves at the Maremma.

Vasilis sat next to me again. I reflected that, no, I had not made a mistake by formulating a hypothetical reason for the flow of history in my century, in which the conclusion was not what was expected; nor was the fruitlessness of my own life pleasant to me. But why did I identify my own biological time with the time of ideas? This identification had not tormented me when I was young. Around me, the world, the ideas, and the expressions were in a state of change, venturing strange consequences. Let them make their own mistakes; and let me take rest finally by saying that the fruitless hypothetical reason for my life had at least served, as much as it could, the needs of my time—as best it could. I still could hear around me the aria broken into pieces by the curt strokes on the keyboard, and I remembered the curt breathing of the woman who the day before had yielded to me in my sleep.

I left before it got dark. I did not want to return home right away. My steps—or perhaps the thought that the time I could devote to walks was diminishing—brought me to the pier. I did not notice that the weather had changed since that morning.

I walked along the length of the empty pier. Some cannons had been driven upside down in the ground. The cables tied around them set the restlessness of the sea next to my feet, lessening it with throbbing movements. The new ship from the Ionian Islands was to arrive the following day. It was just as well that its dark steel mass was not there, because I wanted old times. Dense clouds had lifted the blueness of the waves while laying down their own melancholy. They had hidden the mountains across the way: only a bright stripe unfolded on the horizon, cutting the ash gray in two. The sun slipped through the bright crack, freeing the red colors all at once, from the color of a baby's cheek to the color of pillage.

I stood at the edge of the pier. Speechless in front of the narration that a single color can undertake, indifferent toward the spray that wet my face, I guessed that at that moment my city did not belong to its materiality but to the wishes of another world. I turned and studied it for a long time, until the color of steel chased away all the reds.

I walked up toward my house as the gas lanterns on the main streets were being lit. The first drops of the storm found me outside my door.

I shall inform you about what Vasilis and I talked about in the afternoon: that he wants to give a detailed account of my life in the prologue that he will write. Biography, he said. More specifically, he said that he wanted to shed light on some stages of my life.

After the experience of this evening, I wonder what it means to "shed light" on a life. I fear the narration that a singular biographer undertakes. For example, I sensed that he would attempt to gloss over my financial situation and my unmarried state. To be sure, this will be according to his interpretation, which, I do not doubt, will be accompanied by the best intentions. I listened to him for a long time as he spoke to me about events that did not appeal to me at all. I interrupted him, telling him to do what he thought best—what words, my God, about a life!—with one and only one condition: not to mention a word about our association.

This was the first time that I spoke to him about it—not that he would not have heard; after a certain point, everyone knew, I think. In my own way, I forbade people to talk about it, or even to hint at it. Vasilis answered that he considered it obvious, since I had never till now mentioned your name to him. And he added that he was glad that I entrusted him with the subject, even if I had brought it up by denying him the right to speak about it. Then he asked me what he should do with some other rumors that he happened to have heard about an old engagement. Would I forgive him, he said. Being much younger, and since I did not speak about these things, he had to hear them from a third party. The rumors said that I had become engaged to a wealthy Englishwoman years ago, when I was visiting England. According to what was being said, the engagement had taken place with the prospect that my fiancée would assist the common cause financially—tonight, Louisa, I would say the common hypothetical cause—and that she died in England while I was on a political tour of America that had lasted several months.

This story caused such anxiety in me, as I heard it so unexpectedly, that I was dumbfounded, as if I had lost, along with the words of the orator, the simple voice of humans. I mumbled something presently, I think, again telling him to do whatever he thought best. I managed to add that, if he insisted on that specific subject, he should be especially careful in describing the rumors. I, anyway, I said rather abruptly, had no intention, on such a day and at someone else's home, to begin talking about very private matters. I added that, since I would soon be leaving for Athens, I doubted that we would find time during the following days to discuss these things. Asking him not to misunderstand the lack of time, I begged him to at least not mention anywhere in his prologue the name of the Englishwoman, a name which people very likely knew but I did not want repeated.

I left soon thereafter.

This is how things turn out, Louisa, and here I am, forced to speak on the subject of the Englishwoman as I try to appease the ghosts of my biography. Should I not try to appease you also, since, in reading these pages at some point in time, you will compose a different biography, as truthful and as false as the rest? Once and for all, you should know the following: if I had not been wearing the invisible ring of my engagement with a revolutionary cause (as in fairy tales); if I had not loved you in the way that the embodiment of knowledge and perception so seldom grants us; if, finally—in order to finish with this hypothetical statement—my four-year-long trip in foreign lands was not also (besides being indicative of my concern for the defeat of the uprisings of '48) a parallel, although vain, attempt to forget you, then I would have been in a position to have been linked with the famous Englishwoman.

I'll stop, for the time being, at the last "if." We had just met; it must have been about two years earlier. Let me make it clear that the "just" of tonight had traveled in its time along a slowly drawn curve. It was restrained not only by the fact that you were married but also by my own situation.

When I returned from my studies in Italy, I took over a position as a judge in Nauplion. I soon resigned and returned to Patras. I worked as a lawyer for a time: it was enough to set me on a different course from the man you had married, who was already public prosecutor. I was not interested in any career related to the nonexistent justice of that time. Furthermore, as soon as I set foot here again, I continued my activities against the monarchy with the greatest passion. The fact that the governor of Achaia forbade me from giving the oration on the anniversary of the Revolution in the church of Saint Andrew the first year after my return was not totally unexpected; he must have heard about events in Italy. Besides, my fiery speech, the first speech I gave as an adult in my birthplace, had been printed in Patras and reprinted in neighboring Zakynthos. Do I remember correctly? I did not care, I was saying, for statues but for ideas that unwound the yarn of blood on this harsh landscape until the years of the Achaian Confederacy. The duration of ideas, despite their temporary demise, this is what preoccupied me—because what else could have moved the people of this area to revolt not once or twice but a thousand times. . . .

Let me not repeat what is already familiar, since, when I met you, you had also read the forbidden speech.

So the first spring after my return was fateful in every way. It had more or less forewarned me early on with especially clear days and strong scents. I was waiting for something important to happen. The restriction against speaking in church came. That was not enough. I sensed something deeper, invisible, and fateful.

Even the mansion on Mezonos Street forewarned me as I was entering that everything I set my eyes on that marked night of the dance would remain unfaded. There were flowers for those in love and for the dead in the garlands that decorated the open windows and the entrance. Women with the light of candles flickering tentatively on their bare shoulders were nevertheless certain of the light of an Italian smile on their lips. One man with a violin, another with a clarinet, and a third with a contrabass, all of them wearing tailcoats, crossed for a moment the crowded room to go out to the garden, just a moment before Cupid's arrow crossed the darkness to penetrate my chest.

I had seen you.

I observed the gentleman who accompanied you. I was assured that he was the friend and fellow student of old. He greeted me wholeheartedly and introduced me to his wife. I bowed. My right hand covered the irregular beating of my heart. But I did not retreat. On the contrary, I began to converse with your escort. He was pleasant in company, as I knew him to be, with the sharpness of mind necessary for his aspirations. Having already realized that, to gain fame, he had to get involved with major problems, he had turned decidedly against highway robbery. Besides being unquestionably correct, his move was certainly safer than turning against a dictatorial king. I had heard that in Mesolongi he carried out justice without mercy, being deaf to everything except the promises of his superiors, and detaching from the reprehensible act—I am not objecting—every other dimension except the criminal. He proposed the most weighty sentences. His harshness would not have surprised me if I did not remember that a few years earlier he was different. He continued to be friendly with me, apparently forgetting that I might remember—or perhaps exactly for this reason? I admit that the period we spent together as students, which went by so quickly, made me take a liking to him also, in spite of all that separated us. Let me not exaggerate, however, and let me return to the magic of the spring night.

The dancing had not started yet. With the vanity of a newlywed, your husband led you to a gathering of women. He found me again, and we proceeded to a group of men. All were speaking heatedly because the turmoil that had just started taking shape in Europe, dragging the neighboring Ionian state in its revolutionary maelstrom, influenced financial affairs and ideas everywhere. As for Patras, the second largest city in the Greek kingdom, its close association with the West and with the Heptanesa placed its fate alongside that of other Mediterranean cities in Europe. I am speaking of its way of life, its composition, and its functions. Already, besides its vigorous commercial activity, it had many workshops and mills. A few days before that particular night, the Chamber of Deputies had approved the construction of the first industrial unit in Patras. Land was given to a private citizen for the cultivation of cotton. He was also given the right to build a factory for the production of cotton thread. Thirty young men would be hired to learn how to use and to fix the machines. So the construction of the first factory preoccupied the guests at the dance as much as the situation in Europe, which was pregnant with unrest, balancing their concern about the latter with the optimistic prospect of the former—provided, of course, that the unrest and the economic crisis that usually follows it would not put a stop to everything.

These, anyway, are the things I heard around me, along with efforts at predictions. We, the insiders among the educated, the landowners, the merchants, and the intellectuals of the city, spoke in such a way that our basic disagreement would not be apparent; however, neither would we give the impression of a substantial agreement. I cannot argue that, in the vision of that period in time—I write to you primarily about my own Greek visions, Louisa—the townspeople did not have an important place. Since then the plot has changed: many maintain that no idea stays firm in the flow of time. It is possible that they are right, even though this cannot be substantiated.

I know that—perhaps I have already written to you about this—I do not have time to see if I was right or wrong, not even on the subject of art. I sometimes think that perhaps ideas know that we are monotonously transient, which is why they give us only one lock of their voluptuous hair. They think that is enough: let the brief objections of the passersby dissolve in its recollection, as in a strong acid. I am grateful for, but I do not desire, the slightest gift—no matter how wonderful. If pleasure is legitimate, our doubt about it should also be legitimate: something that I shall not call remorse or mistake. Otherwise, I had no reason to begin this manuscript—if down deep I had no doubts about self-sufficient revolutionaries, self-sufficient writers, and self-sufficient lovers.

The musicians stopped tuning their instruments in the garden. The groups dissolved in the pleasantness—certainly not in the acid—of the melody, leaving the politics of the day unclarified for the time being. Waltz, polka, mazurka, gallop, cotillion—no objection. We danced several times. Each time I asked for the permission of your escort, both for reasons of protocol and with the hope that he would refuse with some excuse. He never refused, advising you gaily to beware of the beautiful words of an orator and a poet. You responded with the smile of a woman who wants to show that she is happy with her marriage. In some way you were, and you would continue to be. I think extremely highly of you because you never stopped loving your mate.

Since that evening you loved him in a different way, you insisted later on, and avoided naming the way. As for the two of us—if my words can still mean something—nothing was repetitive, yet nothing was unprecedented in the way we were overtaken by love. As lovers we grew old examining almost exclusively the materiality of tension, while an opposite, undramatic materiality solidified our life between two meetings. The passion we shared, which I shall not call unjustified, sometimes stretched our words like masks over our countenances. The result of circumstances? It does not matter: the one condemned to the lack of continuity in love serves the sentence of his imagination.

I am thinking that, perhaps, with all these things I am saying, I want to tell you this: the defeat of love has taught me what its triumph would have meant. The defeat of the uprisings also tried to teach me about their triumphs. However, Louisa, how much can teachings and unattainable triumphs teach us?

The thoughts of a cold Christmas night when I am suffering for lack of the comforting warmth of a hay-laden manger. Until I write to you again tomorrow, Louisa, I shall not renounce my romanticism. I speak for the dismissal of old contracts, the observation of nature and the identification with it, the breath of infinity in the finite, the imagination that dwells in our materiality, the chaotic contradictions, the idealization of love and of death. For all these reasons, I do not renounce the way I loved you—even if I throw your letters in the fire, old wooden fragments of a shipwreck. Perhaps from the same ship that was the manger of my own birth? It seems like I am awake, looking at the continuity of an interrupted dream, in which I take part from a great distance. I do not want to wake up; nor do I have time, since in a few days my dream becomes a hundred years old.

In which manger might the "I" of the poor have been born?

Good night. Allow me to guide the boat of your sleep carefully between the reeds and the rushes of the Maremma. Darkness, as is appropriate for big trips. Keep giving me courage. And I shall lull you to sleep by telling you the story of an old countess.

Louisa, the stars on winter journeys are so few.

26 december 1888
patras

Louisa, I postponed my trip to Athens for a few days to take care of some unfinished business; but I did buy a ticket. I shall travel by train.

I'd better not tell you lies. I thought of staying here a little longer to be able to write to you in a quieter environment. If I arrive in Athens earlier, other things will preoccupy me, I feel. I do not have even a room of my own there, and I resort to finding lodging in hotels.

What had kept me away from the field of battle in European cities, leaving only the melancholy of defeat that I felt when I later traveled there? The fear of blood, which is normal even among the bravest intellectuals? The fear that the ideas might turn insane since, during extraordinary events, they can gallop away, dragging every previous formulation to unknown paths? Or perhaps the promise of another type of revolution in the eyes of a desirable woman?

Such questions often bring along their answers. A portion of truth is hidden in each answer, just as a portion of the truth of an idea is hidden in every formulation. I am writing to you then that, in Greece too, an attempt was made to arouse the people. The attempt did not succeed, did not reach an eruption worth commemorating. In the meantime, the European uprisings were brought to the port of Patras, resulting in the suspension of foreign credit and a huge financial crisis that put a stop to the smooth execution of financial obligations to the bank. The flower garlands and dances had definitely become something of the past, as you probably remember. The following year, the first Italian refugees began to arrive in Athens, the first defeated revolutionaries, these desperate firstborn children of freedom, as an Athenian newspaper called them.

Most of them were Italians, but there were also Poles and Hungarians. The Kanaris government refused to deport them, and the Chamber of Deputies approved a request for assistance. The Austrian ambassador's objections that neutrality had been violated, which provoked objections from other nations as well, and especially the sight of the ragged, armed, and unemployed followers of Garibaldi, did not take long to dampen the initial enthusiasm and to bring a stop to the assistance program. An order was given for their disarmament, and no more visas were issued to "beggars and idle people who were practicing no occupation" to go to Athens. Ten years later, on the death of General Riccardi, perhaps the best known of the political refugees after the defeat of '48, the newspapers in Patras wrote that he died a stranger, isolated from relatives and friends. That same year the new struggle of the Italians against the Austrians brought about the return of quite a few fugitives, a return that soon became complete when the unification of Italy allowed their repatriation.

Patras, more so than other cities, assisted them during their passage or their permanent establishment. Here, everyone who had anything to do with education or business spoke Italian. The old fighters were still living. Among them were many who had fled to the Ionian Islands or to Italy during the course of the War of Independence. Besides, quite a few families, including mine, had followed the same path. Now our fate was echoed in the arrival of the new refugees, giving the debtors a chance to pay their debts in this life without the interest of posthumous judgment. Independent of the various explanations, the arrival of the first refugees, a captain and sixty-nine soldiers from the garrison of Ancona, caused a sensation. The governor himself welcomed them and gave an order for lodging to be found. Some time later, about the same number came from the garrison of Rome by way of Corfu. With them were General Riccardi, other officers, young men of different occupations, as well as twelve women. It was still the beginning; Othon himself contributed from his personal treasury, and in many Greek cities committees were formed to assist the fugitives who were undesirable in Europe.

I participated in their relief as much as I could. The ruin of individuals (and of our ideas in Italy) depressed me also. As I talked to them, the thought that I had to act quickly and bypass the speed of events matured within me. I was ashamed that I had not been there at the roadblocks even though—as I wrote to you—we had some prospects over here. I saw traitors—should I call them traitors? One night I dreamed of Mazzini himself, the fiery leader of the Italian Revolution: I dreamed that he came to my house and was asking me to hide him in Patras until morning, when he would depart. I assumed that he would escape to Switzerland, as he had done in the past, and that he would be deported from there once again. I had never seen him face-to-face. While living in Italy, I, naturally, did not happen to meet the famous *carbonaro,* the founder of "Young Italy." Nor was a picture of his face anywhere. I just had the feeling that his name flew low, as birds tend to do before a storm, while his unknown face was described as fiery, as were his political articles. I did not know him, yet his face seemed tired in my dream. Perhaps because I had learned from his persecuted followers that he was of sickly temperament and that he was crushed, on the one hand, by the defeat of Milan, where he had hurried from abroad and was forced to leave again very quickly, and, on the other, by the fall of Rome, where he had also hurried and, as a member of the triumvirate, had defended the city against the French troops. No one knew where he had been wandering since. Then it happened that I dreamed of him. In any case, the routes of the persecuted are verified much later, if they are ever verified.

What I called destination again claimed me like an unforeseen love. Was this also a syndrome of defeat? I had to establish closer and more permanent connections with the international organizations. I had to draw certain conclusions. I had to see the blood on the wound before it thickens and becomes ink.

That is when my father died. All the old as well as the new families of landowners, businessmen, and politicians, with our substantial extended family in the lead, accompanied the gentle old man, praising him for not having fallen prey to postrevolutionary heroics—they avoided saying to the material and symbolic profiteering that followed the liberation. I did not believe in the sincerity of their praises. Personally, I respected him for many things. For instance, his decision not to marry again must have been very hard on him. He belonged to the large category of those who cannot express their feelings in any way other than ritualistically: engagement, wedding, grief. He did not budge from the thought of his dead wife, keeping the same sternness and silence he had kept during the years he lived with her. However, with her and separate from her, he appeared self-sufficient. I envied him and loved him for the self-sufficiency he showed either because of modesty or in order not to weigh others down with his problems.

Breaching etiquette, you took off your glove for a moment and placed your hand in my palm.

I had to grow old before I, like the supreme fatalist, came to the conclusion that when two hands, trembling, meet for the first time and come to an understanding of a pact between them, their love is doomed. One is deluded into thinking that it does not seem possible for a condemnation to begin with the need for touching, with the grasping of two hands. Yet, tonight let me wonder, Louisa, whether the hand that waved the sheer tulle over the candles, the tears, the flower arrangements, the people, was your hand: the one that compelled the contours to fade away in their halo; the chants, to the opposite shore; and all the movements to take on the grace of a slow, endless caress. Let me wonder.

Because, although at noon I held a magic hand, late in the evening I was overtaken by the thought that I would have to start practicing law again. In order to make the thought more attractive, I added harmless political activity to the practice of law. I had to earn money to be able to contend for you on equal terms. However, despite the fact that your marriage had brought me to these thoughts, not for a moment did I think of marrying you—only of vying for you. Besides, it would have been impossible for you to get a divorce. The grasping of our hands promised another type of ring; we both knew it.

Later that same evening, I had on my lips, along with your true name, the taste of a strange freedom that the death of a father gives a young man. I would miss his discreet admonitions, since from then on I could literally and totally go to waste pursuing the most unselfish dreams. On the other hand, I was distressed by the fact that, just when I welcomed the independence sons are destined to have, the desire for a woman who was not to be taken came to squeeze me tightly with the rope of another type of bondage. It was not your marriage that scared me, as you often claimed, but the realization of the loneliness that would follow the onset of this love. Would it be different than my father's?

It was almost dawn when I decided that I would follow the path of my solitary life till the end. To make a long story short, Louisa, that evening I decided to draw up the contract whereby I would distance myself from my inheritance, the little of it that was left—in order to enter the morrow with the sanctity of the naked, I used to say—and thus to be accepted by you, if it were meant for us to be joined together. This decision, it seems, was my only defense against the onset of desire. At the same time I decided—how many times are you willing to forgive my use of this verb?—to leave Greece as soon as possible in order to make our defeat known abroad. Were we not perchance also defeated? I was anxious to take new oaths and to become involved in whatever was already becoming apparent, that is, in the prospect of a Pan-European union of nations: as a Greek, a quality that still carried some value for the European spirit; and as a poet and public speaker, qualities that time would assign to their place in the light or the darkness. In the decisions of that sleepless night was the core of all my ideas, which from that time on I would develop in my most important speeches, articles, and dramatic works.

One more time: do you understand why I never spoke or wrote about our love?

I maintain that our separation that night was deeper than any of our later true separations. Touching your bold hand, I swore to love it and to refuse it. Our relationship was cultivated in the sand of this contradiction. The following day I tried to meet you. We soon met. You know all this. Secretly, however, I was preparing my big trip to foreign lands, and thus a few months went by.

I remember our first meetings. You ask what do I remember? The stretched rope of danger; the new glossary of bodies; the magnificence of a common delusion; the acceptance of whatever goodness had not been committed to your marriage; your words—that you had thought of me in your imagination and waited for me; that you soon said "forever"; that I wanted to give you eternity in return, as I was obliged to do in view of our daring and our feelings, but I feared your tender enslavement.

Once I confided in you that I was planning to leave without saying much about the purpose of the trip. I told you something about the new ideas and the devotion they demanded.

You already knew about them since you had read my banned speech. You added that since then you read anything relevant that fell in your hands (not too many things, to be sure) and came to the conclusion that these ideas appeared to you to be generally correct.

You could not yet see (or am I mistaken, perhaps?) behind the printed words the extent of my political aspirations and their rivalry with my aspirations regarding you—nor the ragged glove that the last defeated individual tossed to me as he was exiting from the empty European stage.

I stayed away from you about four years, traveling around the Old Continent and the New World. The times demanded that I often wear the national costume of my country. National consciousness played an important role in the projected revolutions of those who were not yet liberated, in the creation of national independent nations, and in the Pan-European union. I was referring directly to the way in which the Westerners had imagined and idealized us, moved by the Revolution that had taken place thirty years earlier. I provoked strong impressions. As usually happens with similar provocations, our people supported them, and the opponents ridiculed them. I am sure, for instance, that if Vasilis draws on friendly descriptions, he will present me in the biography that he is preparing with expressions such as "in his blossoming years . . . the sweet clarity of his blue eyes, their penetrating and imposing quality . . . the rich and magnificent national costume with the *foustanela* and the gold-trimmed vest and leggings . . . spread an angelic charm and glamour. . . ." This positive exaggeration will be modified if the opinions of my political opponents are someday included in their improvised autobiographies. I write this to you, Louisa, because, while I was in London, I heard that a wealthy young man of letters, who had just come from Ermoupolis to London—to stay thereon—described my speech to city hall as follows: "He appeared on the podium shaking his long hair and holding in his left hand the large thick pages of his manuscript. The English, used to hearing their orators speaking extemporaneously and not reading their speeches, waited with curiosity for the commencement of the reading. However, the pronunciation of the speaker was so strange that I doubt if anyone was able to understand a word of the long speech." It seems that the attempt of some to present me in a ludicrous manner had begun. Since then, the process of making me the subject of lampoonery, based mostly, I believe, on my decision to refuse everything conventional, was an attempt to undermine my position, both as a politician and as a poet. It was not so difficult: having written works for the theater, I know it well. It is a good thing that the most noble knight, Don Quixote, with whose name they honored me many times, thinking that they were ridiculing me, never lived in Albion. I shall not refrain from writing to you also, Louisa, that the articles printed in the *Eastern Star*, which was published by a politician and philhellene named Covden, were full of praise for me and that, naturally, I did not answer the critical comments, for it is self-evident that my knowledge of English was limited, while I spoke and wrote Italian and French with ease.

Finally, I have to speak to you in greater detail about the purpose of that trip. Despite its failure, do not discuss the things that I shall tell you with anyone, since they are related to acts that do not concern only me. I also trust that you will destroy these pages.

Two years after the burst of uprisings in Europe and shortly after their failure, an international organization was established in London under the name European Democratic Central Committee. Its purpose was twofold: on the one hand, to form national chapters in every country; on the other, to spread the idea of a European democratic federation that would be comprised of independent, democratically run national states. These would result from nationalist and socialist uprisings. However, since the uprisings that were to follow did not seem to proceed with any urgency—how could they after the general defeat?—the committee raised some funds, printed some newspapers, and stopped functioning after three years.

I represented Greece and observed the activities of the committee, which was inspired by Mazzini's revolutionary vision. I should tell you that the defeated leader had fled to London. There he toiled to form an alliance of people so powerful that it would be able to measure up to the Holy Alliance and shatter it. I came face-to-face with him for the first time. His appearance was different than in my dream, when he begged me for refuge in Patras. He seemed calmer, despite the harshness that had come over his Mediterranean consonants. Since I started writing to you of the above, let it be known that France was represented by the democratic leader Ledru-Rollin and Germany by the revolutionary Rüge. Wherever this last one appeared, he was always accompanied by the rumor of his friendship with the very well known, in certain circles, Karl Marx. There were also Romanians, Poles, and various others. As a matter of fact, some Romanians and some Italians, I think, all members of the committee, were previously refugees in Athens and had decided to publish a newspaper, an event that speeded their deportation from Greece. Useful ideas for thinking people regarding the liberation movements in southern and eastern Europe, most of which came into being during the French Revolution, would appear a little later in the newspaper that I published as soon as I returned.

For the time being, Louisa, I shall return to the events that took place during my stay in Europe. Parenthetically, I would like to underline my concern that I might not have time to write to you about the things that surface, flooding me in bursts of waves. I am thinking, however, about the worth of my own emotional—and, consequently, insolvent—view of my life, even if it is directed only toward you. At least it is not self-serving autobiography. Friendship perhaps, offered to our love story. That is why I would like you to do me the favor of reading these pages in the future, before you destroy them.

Yes, I accepted the wedding proposal sent to me by the Englishwoman. Yesterday I touched briefly on the reasons that prevented my heart as well as my hand from appearing eager when I signed the prenuptial agreement. It stated that, after the wedding, I would have a yearly income of a thousand pounds from the bride's dowry. The wedding ceremony was scheduled to take place after I returned from America, where I had to go as soon as possible because of the needs of the committee.

Do you find it logical for me to be signing such agreements when, not long before, again by signing a contract, I had distanced myself from my inheritance? Louisa, look at this contradiction with the discernment of time that does not turn back and for this reason is compassionate toward us. I do not deny it; her proposal flattered many of my ambitions, which had flared up as I found myself among people who had led revolutions, or were about to lead in revolutions to come. The Englishwoman appeared to have a liking for me and for our ideas. Her own idea with respect to Greece was derived from an extreme, but old-fashioned by now, sense of Byronism—to which I contributed with my national costume—without its pain obviously. I could not refuse her proposal, especially when my new friends became excited about the money that would support our work. All my earnings would go toward the well-known debt to Mazzini. Thus, I accepted.

How else could I explain to you that it was very easy for this cause to become the love of my life? Not even for a tiny moment was I in love with her, even though love is not the most necessary prerequisite for marriage. Even if this engagement were in keeping with the resplendent atmosphere of big cities and with our dark plans, even if it were in keeping, furthermore, with examples of such weddings in the Ionian Islands and in Patras, in no way could it have been in keeping with the meaning that Greece, Italy, and Anatolia had for me. The Englishwoman did not understand my soul. I assume, in giving so much money, she certainly would not have wanted to face the disability of the statues. What would the word "Maremma" have brought to her mind, even if she had read Dante with the greatest studiousness? As a young man in Italy—I shall not write again "unbelievably young"—I thought that I would not get involved with any woman but the one who would be just as anxious about my ideas as I was. This did not happen with my acquaintances there, nor, more to the point, did I conjure up the logic of my youth when I saw you. Suddenly, you gave flesh and bones to the most primitive, to the erotic I want to say, vision of a lonely man. Suddenly, I grew up. I am still grateful to you.

The last argument: I could have married my fiancée, and the honeymoon could have coincided with my trip to America. However, I indicated that I wanted to visit the New World alone. I claim, therefore, that I resisted the proposal and, even more so, its becoming a reality by taking refuge in the intervention of time. The patriotic reasons did not convince me completely as to the necessity of the wedding, and I dropped words to this effect in conversations with my friends. But I did not have too much time for conversation, as I was leaving for America.

I believe I have told you about crossing the stormy Atlantic in a warship, my welcome by the mayor of New York and the Greek community, my visits and speeches in large cities, my connections with American philhellenes. Niagara Falls aroused great awe in me. I would describe it many times, years later, in the scholarly circles of Athenian salons. I shall not repeat what you already know, limiting myself instead to the feeling, permanent since then (a feeling that I have also mentioned in publications), that the new continent had the old one as a point of departure but was set apart from it by the daring and the speed of its own exemplary youthfulness. Its revolution had consecrated it next to the French and the Greek Revolutions. I arrived at the conclusion that, of the three revolutions, the Greek pressed forward the brotherhood of peoples; the American, the equality of peoples of one race; and the French sought the triumph of individual freedom and the freedom of all the world. Dedicated to the calling of my times, I formulated the celebrated sentence *"Revolution is the law of progress."*

A year went by, and I reembarked to return to Europe. The weather this time was good. The ocean in its turn took me on a journey of all the ways infinity devises to appear to us, the passersby—if and as it appears. Upon my arrival, I avoided going directly to London. I spent quite a few months in Paris. I had decided not to marry the Englishwoman for the very simple reason that I had not stopped thinking about you even for a minute—though this may be an exaggeration to offset my guilt. The few but very warm letters that we exchanged during my absence also helped. It is time to write this to you also: I had asked my fiancée that we not correspond during the time I was going to be away. So you can bask in the thought that I took the overseas trip with you.

As for the rest, let the biographers deal with it.

I began to realize that the ideas of the French Revolution first came to an end in 1848. I belonged to the generation that, having the privilege of distance created by a few decades (but also for other reasons difficult to explain), pretended not to see the deflection of the Revolution by dealing with its ethics and the logic of its causes. Those were the years when I still thought that ideas can be diverted and can later expunge their deviation with impunity. The only thing that remains for me to hold tightly in my hand is the seed that does not promise the same tree. I ask myself which tree. Nothing more optimistic.

I shall end by writing to you that, after the defeat of the uprisings, there was something like a conclusion, even though it already existed as an indefinite idea: that freedom and the formation of national states would result from the dissolution of three empires—the Ottoman, the Austro-Hungarian, and the Russian—not so that the world would become (literally) full of small, weak states but so that all of them together would form their own free federation, a European federation of democratic states. We maintained that if a nation was not incorporated into a broader mosaic, it would soon end up inflexible and tyrannical. Our aim was the creation of the so-called New Europe, a name that also had its prehistory. The educated, the men of letters, the artists, and the vocational classes were all, more or less, for the idea of one ecumenical nationalism. The well-to-do did not go along with this, unless their country had splintered off into warring factions, which made the movement of money difficult.

If, in my time, the artists and intellectuals of the West showed no proof of their education besides letting their palms linger tenderly over marble sculptures and their eyes linger reflectively on the crests of waves, I attempted the opposite movement, not only once but twice. I wanted, I repeat, to see people close up, people who could elicit even from a poor man or a farmer the wish to die for an idea formulated in their books. Whether the poor knew how to read or not did not interest death. Furthermore, I had understood that not long after the blood freezes and turns into ink, it becomes warm blood once again. What type of magician was hiding behind the repeated metamorphoses? Yes, I wanted to see his face behind the mask of pages—to converse, if possible, and to learn.

My trip of initiation would never allow me to call upon the self-sufficiency and the peace of my provincialism in the future. Words such as "happy" or "unhappy," "sick" or "healthy," "poor" or "rich," "single" or "married," were ascribed, in no uncertain terms, to the long-departed vocabulary of a kindly provincialism. Once more, I would have no other country except the world of ideas, and, simultaneously, I would be the most fervent worshiper of my country. My life and my work would be obliged not to be at odds from then on, but, orchestrated to my puritanism, to be more harmoniously compatible.

It is obvious that there was no room for much else. Intentionally, I considered certain wishes secondary in order to reject them more easily. However, my longing for you was enlisted in the search of the purest, the ideal, the absolute. My love was not in contradiction with the puritan revolutionary spirit that possessed me; on the contrary, I had become more sensuous. Along with all this, I used to say that if death did not favor me in an uprising, it should at least be symbolic. Nothing could be left to chance anymore, or appear to be left to chance, since I advocated a logical explanation, even if it were insane, about the birth of history. Love always had its own strong determinism that excluded it from the fortuitous.

All in all, I was able to endure in some areas but not in others. What should I measure?

We met again. Again the same arrow.

The years of fair weather in love coincided with the years of my most intense antiroyalist activity. I was happy; tonight I dare pull this word out of my long-departed provincial vocabulary, not having any other less ambiguous way to specify time, even if I exaggerate somewhat in its assessment. Besides, for quite some time, good and bad have belonged to the two curvatures of the same magnifying glass.

At about that time I wrote my last poems. I had seen that poetry, despite its many masks, had no other course but the path of an interiorized love, and I was frightened.

27 december 1888
patras

I am still in Patras and still writing to you. What madness! I should be able to finish, however. I hope the firewood will last, because it is very cold, and I have a fire burning constantly.

Last night it snowed. In the morning I saw snow everywhere: the aria of nature for the death of a single summer afternoon—for a most distant love; its aria for a shape that is tormented but unable either to come to life or to die out on the whiteness—as the dead and loved ones visit us.

No, it does not snow here often.

We did not meet often, either because of your responsibilities as a married woman or because I had very little free time. The bilingual newspaper which I started publishing in Patras and later in Athens with the title *I Ellinikí Siméa—Le Drapeau Hellénique* demanded all my attention. I wrote most of the articles. In this newspaper I also published my last poems. At the present time, I do not have any issue at hand; do you, by any chance, have any?

I shall write a couple of words about it so all that activity will not be lost, since, I am afraid, the issues of that militant newspaper have been lost. Vanity? Do not fall in the trap of answering.

My articles were based on the enlightenment I had derived

from my international experience. I tried to proceed in my country using this experience as my guide. The French language gave my newspaper an audience beyond the Greek terrain. I used to mail it to many European intellectuals and politicians; it was sent as far as America. I shall mention two instances: I sent the first ten issues to Victor Hugo, along with a letter; I also sent the newspaper to Edgar Quinet, with whom I began a correspondence that lasted many years. I hope that the vicissitudes in the lives of these two men, both of them exiled at that time by Napoleon III, will still allow them to salvage a few tokens of their writings, even though my life has been deprived of what was its own. However, I commanded the sharp memory of poets, sharper yet when their poetic art is close to drying up. As a conspirator, I had to cultivate it as much as possible.

I shall entrust to you, then, whatever I remember. Even if a few issues have been salvaged, I am afraid that they may get destroyed at some point in time by a natural disaster—even worse, by indifferent or enemy hands.

For two years I dedicated myself to the writing and the publishing of the newspaper. I put aside only two or three hours in the afternoon for correspondence—hours during which I allowed myself to think of you also. During the first summer, I remember, the summer wind, the *meltémi*, did not blow at all to hinder the perpendicular rays that kept me company as they fell from the skylight to the floor next to my desk. I wrote letters while the city sank in its countless caricatures during its afternoon nap. I memorized Hugo's answer before I printed it in the newspaper. Here are some of his phrases, written in August 1856: "The arrival of your excellent newspaper moves me tremendously. . . . Keep working for the unification of nations. The spirit of Europe must shine today and replace the old spirit of nationalities. . . . It is beautiful for one to be from the place of light and to carry in oneself the flag of liberty. . . ."

Quinet's answer, sent in June, had arrived earlier. From it, as much as I remember of it, I glean the following: "A reminder of the sacred land, two issues of *I Ellinikí Siméa,* here is more than what one needs to forget a whole day of exile! Yes, I loved this land of the gods very much. . . . I cannot help feeling that I am a compatriot of these valleys of Moreas, where I left a very good part of my youth. . . . I have hardly paid back to Greece all I owe her. . . ."

Louisa, I am still moved; why should I hide it? I shall add only a couple of words from my own responses to Quinet—not for posthumous fame but for the style of a period in time that has been lost. I wrote to him how much I had admired him since my early years. I thought of him, even though I had not met him; however, I had read his *Les esclaves* in London. I remember how persistently I had asked him to write about Greece since he had earlier traveled through the Greek lands and had published his impressions. I was interested in his political point of view. I had spoken to him about the Megáli Idéa of a country with Constantinople as its capital and about eight million people still in bondage in Anatolia; about the public works that had been erected in Greece since he had visited; about the character of the recent movements; and about the reduction of brigandage, in spite of the latest cases. For these, conditions at the frontier zone were partly to blame, I wrote to him. These conditions are no indictment against Greece, but they demonstrate that Turkey, by its very nature, always was a form of organized brigandage. I begged him to send me his works because friends had looted my library while I was in Europe. I asked him to tell me how we could correspond without putting ourselves in danger. Finally, in this first letter I sent him, I wrote to him that, instead of using my real name, I would be signing as Loui.

Again I ask myself if in truth I had given you drafts of my letters as well as letters I had received for safekeeping or if this is just a conjecture, persistent as the memory of a lover or the angel of one close to death. Would it be too much trouble for you to throw a glance in your drawer or in your chest? Wish you would find them. Hold on to them.

My next letter was sent out six months later, with the greatest precautions. I informed Quinet that I had been living in Athens for four months already; that the publication of *I Ellinikí Siméa* had been suspended; that I had no hopes it would be coming out again soon; that during the recent occupation of Piraeus, there was, unfortunately, a climate of empathy toward those in government, but they were instruments of the papacy and of Austria ever since they stepped on Greek land; that the constitution was also a farce, for we had neither free elections nor a free press; that the destiny of the nation had become a *bordello*—I wrote the word to him in Italian. . . . But the nation was rising again. The democrats of France had to come to our defense. . . . For the time being, publication of his article in *I Ellinikí Siméa* would be postponed. Was I to continue corresponding with him by way of Mr. Tarrid, the bookkeeper? Was he to be trusted?

As for the last letter I wrote to him at that time, it was angry and melancholy. I confessed my illness (literally and metaphorically—he could draw his own conclusions). I had returned to Athens once again. We were in a state of death: I and a few followers were fighting Satan himself. We were persecuted and harassed. Wished that God would give us courage. . . . The newspaper continued to be suspended, which is why I had written nothing about his works. Some friends had ordered them through bookstores. I asked him for two brochures, for Michelet's address, and for his own.

I waited for you at the outskirts of Patras, at the place called Ities. You pulled the latch of the gate anxiously and ran toward the house. The scarf you had around your hair came loose. A playful wind rolled it away as far as the trunk of a palm tree. Was it the silk of a faithful guardian or an unfaithful traitor? You could not figure it out as you watched it for a moment, which is why you continued to run, deciding that we did not need veils anymore. Perhaps that is why. I saw the statue of your head, a head that tended to take on an infinite number of symbolic meanings. I could not stand their number and turned my glance elsewhere.

I returned to the idea of your beauty—what is the meaning of "beautiful woman"?—when I later caught myself concentrating on your hair, loose on the pillow. I did not want you with infinite symbolic meanings. The number would defeat me decisively; but you continued to send your symbols to the mirror of my naked body. Their reflection returned to your skin to be dissolved in the dew of a very fine perspiration. I breathed the cinnamon of your hair. Every once in a while, a little sob with the word "Maremma" would fall in tune with the reels of your hair. I insisted that you should not leave everything to come with me to Athens. Had you understood that, up to a point, I was telling you lies?—the legitimate lie of one in bondage. Besides, I was not going there for recreation: very generally, I mentioned jobs that I had to take care of and other business. Perhaps I would also have to go into hiding, so I would not be able to have you with me unless I opted to become handicapped. I turned to you and told you that our love had been announced with so many separations that it could not be favored by a specific end. Its flow would be unstoppable, and it would mark our countenance: it is called time. Our love—were my words any comfort to you, Louisa?—constitutes a lifelong idea for the laborers of dreams. That is why everything will be and everything at the same time will come to an end. Think how many times the yarn leading to the exit of the labyrinth must have been cut to be tied together again more tightly—

unless it was not about exiting but about entering the deepest pit of love and death, about the sun outside or the beast in the darkness of the maze, one and the same.

Loose words, like your hair on a pillow. No, I never talked to you this way. These words I could have written to you. A whole lifetime, and I did not find the courage to do it.

Forgive the daring of this moment.

For many reasons I return to more level ground. So I spent the greater part of the following years in Athens. The town of my student days had spread its fine marble buildings on trespassed plans, in the same manner as its contemporary, Patras, the second largest city in Greece. In both cases, I was bothered by the senseless eagerness for whatever was new, although it seems that it cannot be otherwise when there is money. This is not what we had in mind when we were saying that the place had to become modernized for its own sake and for the sake of our ideas. There were times when I agonized over the ease with which visions turn into sleek avenues, especially as the contrast between the two larger cities and the country was becoming more and more pronounced as time went on. From my European experience, I knew that the capital cities everywhere functioned like galleries at the opera—at least their centers did. Even so, Louisa, I liked both the capitals and the melodrama. I mean to say, in Athens I was less in danger of considering myself isolated than I was in the country. In Athens it seemed that friends could be closer together and more devoted, as if the greater number of people made us more daring—and, without doubt, gave us more opportunities for arguments as well. Despite the ceaseless activity, I did not stop frequenting some of the salons in the capital. I soon gained a reputation as an excellent conversationalist and, unavoidably, the affection of women. However, I was possessed by the thought of you. All these people did not see or did not suspect the thorn in the rose of a boutonniere. It's better that they remain in a subtle hue, which had its own power. Ignoring the power of such gatherings would seem naive to me. I think I wrote to you already that many townspeople, mostly businessmen, in both Athens and Patras, as well as elsewhere, funded our organizations and our publications and sometimes assisted anyone in need of money. No one among them considered his donation as pardon for his wealth, which we would not have given very easily. Our long-standing and often fruitful alliances were based on other issues. However, this is not of interest at this moment.

In the letters you sent me at the time, you wrote that you were trying to understand my ideas by reading newspapers and books and that you met up with me in quite a few instances. I used to think that, yes, on the one hand, you were also imprisoned, but you stuck your hand outside the bars of your imprisonment until you reached my impoverishment, touching me generously always.

You had devised a code in your letters. I do not insist that it was unbroken. When I wrote to you in jest that it committed me to white magic, you answered that women in love always charm their sacred illness with the help of magic. It did not matter if the magic emanates from within or from a change in the world without. It did matter that these charmers, dressed in the beautiful dresses of women in love, walked on trees and on roof tiles like a patch of light in the clouds.

Louisa, you had me and you held on to me. How much I longed for you and how much you shocked me with the things you wrote to me in some such manner! One day I caught myself following unconsciously a patch of light that was moving ahead of me on some street in Athens.

I had a need to feel that I was in love.

Another day I asked myself to what extent the same magic could travel through the spine of my revolutionary talk. I had no answer for the forged question.

I want to write to you that those years were among the most important of my life—not because I was younger, which was more or less insignificant in view of the fact that I was in love, but because I had acquired my own dead. I do not mean parents and kin; I mean the others, for whom, as you know, I spoke many times "on behalf of all." I do not limit the "on behalf of all" to the citizens of Patras or of Athens. In the crowd of those gathered stood the souls of others, from other periods of time. All around, bouquets of flowers overflowed with the promised freedom, and so did we, the living, with old and new oaths. If the dead dream of the living, we had to respond to a dream of victory, which would bring rest to them. I am wondering to what degree, with the refined wisdom of their dreams, they were aware of the Maremma of whatever victory and for this reason kept politely quiet.

They say that I was the best orator of my time. I cannot have an opinion. Organizations and private citizens called on me to bid good-bye to the bigwigs. My funeral orations were printed right away, as was the case with the rest of my speeches. I shall confide a detail to you: it happened sometimes, just before I started to speak and as I was concentrating, that the scarf from the head of a woman who ran to embrace me would slide off. The silk scarf would spread out over those gathered—reminiscent of the way Westerners painted the Holy Spirit floating over the heads of those called to be apostles. I was afraid that someone would see its tassels caressing my gray hair as the hand—so distant now—of Kapodistrias stroked my childhood locks. I was about forty years old, and I was the predestined one, the lamb, and the man in love with you. Even though it is late, I have to thank you, I think, for the caress with which you inspired me in difficult public times.

I had such a need to feel in love.

Although when I was younger I used to write verses to our country and to love, joining the two rather unskillfully, and although later on only the hand of the country knocked on my deficient lyre, I soon stopped writing poetry. I think I mentioned it to you above—that I published my last poems in *I Ellinikí Siméa* and that I still have in front of me some old manuscripts. I do not want any of these to be left around. I would like to ask you, if you still have old issues of the newspaper, to destroy my verses—I do not care how you do it. But again I say, is it possible for me to ask you for my blood, in the name of another period in time or in the name of my deficiency?

Was it the times perhaps? Did you exert control over the way I wrote? Was I afraid that some word would betray us? If I have not lost all reason due to the speed of time—I took out of my vest pocket my silver watch, a gift from you: quarter of three—I can claim that publicly I never was more tender than I was during those antiroyalist funeral orations.

It was not just the silk of your touch that made me tender nor the attraction that the idea of death exerts on a romanticist. What happened was what usually happens, more or less, when eyes are tearful: the picture of the world became humanized inside the broken pane of tears—as if there can be no idea, Louisa, without the need for dead flesh to be clothed, no immortality without the need of a grave, and no man without the need to be remembered by a woman.

28 december 1888
patras

Dawn of the twenty-eighth. I am trying to write to you continuously and not go out at all, except when necessary. This does not mean that I am able to write more. Besides, this is my last day in Patras. Tomorrow I shall go to Athens. I have not slept well. I was cold and kept waking up. I was waiting for daybreak—so I could dream of you again, after abandoning myself to the dream of writing.

It is not a river. Something like a Maremma, but full of words with closed eyelids.

I see you smiling because, in speaking to you yesterday about the invisible aspects of funeral speeches, I did not refrain from referring to my own sleep even though it was early in the morning. One may suspect that all these days and nights I was doing nothing other than composing my own funeral oration. Louisa, for the sake of a past embrace, swear to be good to me. I am writing to you in no uncertain terms that I do not have such an intention. I, the mystic of funeral orations, do not want a grave or orations. The times rather favor silence.

But I shall not silence at least one event. I am of the opinion that between two periods of time that are very close, there can be a huge difference in the way people live and in the way they die, just as there is in the rhetoric or in the silence of the one and the other. That is why I do not intend to use new words;

I shall return to the rhetoric of thirty years ago by gleaning excerpts from the funeral oration for Nikolaos Makriyannis, the son of the general: August, at the cemetery of Athens, two years before the dethronement of Othon. My speech was published in *To Méllon tis Patrídos*. I left an offprint with Panayiotis. I have another here, from which I copy the following:

> . . . *Yesterday, after midnight, I received a letter, with which the respected family of the former general, General Makriyannis, in announcing the death of the son lying before us, asked me at the same time to say a few words at the grave site as a last farewell. Who in all of Greece does not know the infinite number of tribulations, who has not been touched by the pain and the sorrows of the venerable soldier Makriyannis and his family? . . .*
>
> *This family . . . a living cluster of Laocoon. . . . Laocoon, however, of the East? . . . Our much-suffering people? . . .*
>
> *And I confess to you, Sirs, with great sorrow, but clearly and sincerely: I did not wish to go up to the graves anymore, I did not wish to raise my voice anymore. If I were not afraid that I would distress the grieving father, the respectable Makriyannis, I would have turned a deaf ear toward his kind invitation and I, too, would have come with the grief locked up in my heart, but with voiceless lips, like one of those dark nights on the ocean, when sky and air and sea appear in deep silence but embody terrible storm! . . .*
>
> *When in a nation . . . freedom is mocked, patriotic speech is barred . . . it is not worth grieving for the dead one . . . he is saved, freed, like the nightingale that leaves its cage, in which it was locked up. . . .*
>
> *I wanted to withdraw to the life-giving desert of nature, I wanted to leave and go far away to foreign lands, if my duty toward my country had not contravened. Life for me is the fulfillment of one's duty, and I never want to fail in my duty, although I know that my suffering is already sterile! Is there any one among you who has kept the divine flame in his soul and does not feel likewise?*

> *For the evil ones there is even on this earth, and, as a matter of fact, continuously, the day of the last judgment. We see it in the great theater of history, and woe to those who scorn the teachings of history! . . .*
>
> *Our glorious Revolution became as Makriyannis himself: a ghost! . . . It is you, oh, glorious elder, unblemished fighter of 1821 and 1843! Your torments are bitter, and your pain is great; but take comfort, you, the mighty one in virtue, the mighty one in war . . . accept the warm tears and the sincere love of the new generation and of all the people of Greece. . . .*

The years would pass, I would write my two dramatic works, and even then—why do I say then? Until today, the puzzle of history took hold of me with the power of a drug. In my works love was youthful, idealized, and, after many trials, ended in happiness; still, I knew very well that life does not allow such oversimplifications. Politics, however, was a dirty business, just as it is in reality. Without identifying history with politics, I had the sense that *"the great theater of history,"* which I emphasized in front of the general, had been transmitted in some way to my theatrical works. Why, then, did I describe love differently than I knew it and lived it?—a question which, as you know, was inevitably asked once.

Part of the mistake that took control of my life, if I can call something a mistake, is that I was not able to decide conclusively on my position either toward love or—I dare say—toward history and especially toward the theater between them. Was I an interpreter, was I a spectator, was I a creator? Look: what natural or divine law brought the unblemished Makriyannis and me together three times, all of which were significant to me? The first time, when as a young man he stood on the dock at the time of my birth, sword in hand. The second, when, with two other generals, he accompanied Kapodistrias on his trip through Patras. (Did I write to you about that? He had been present during my initiation to oratory.) The third, when I spoke at the funeral of his son.

I mean to say, what is theater?

Outside the city is stirring. It is immersing itself in the self-sufficiency of the next twenty-four hours. The shops must have opened by now. I shall send word to have some food and some firewood delivered. If I go out, I am afraid that I might not find you on my return.

As I bring to mind all my unwritten life, it seems to take on—first my life itself and then the recording of it—the features of dreams. For this reason, I say that as one grows old or comes out of a deep dream, he has the feeling that only half of something stays with him, regardless of whether that something has made its own circle either in life or in the course of one night.

A wounded man on the shore of a lake, unable to reach the redeeming water—if, of course, there is water—wounded and wrapped in my Italian cape. It was then, I believe, that I was photographed. Just as a fairy tale assigns to the king his fur coat, to the refugee his rags, and to the beloved her complexion, in the same way I was of the opinion that I should surround my image forever with this old-fashioned piece of clothing.

Wide, folded-over collar. The beautiful lips of one in love, or perhaps the merciless lips of an orator? Nothing changes if you change the adjectives and say the beautiful lips of an orator and the merciless lips of one in love. Twisted mustache, bare chin, long curly hair—it had started to get thinner near the forehead. Deep eyes.

I lived in Athens most of the time. Many times I used to come down to Patras for conspiratorial reasons. Once in a while I would meet with you. Your husband was often away in Mesolongi. His toughness as a public prosecutor had become the nightmare of the bandits during their night outings and during their daytime sleep—not that I was sympathetic to the gang leaders, the deserters, and the bandits. Nor would I have opened up the subject if it had not touched our lives in different ways for each of us. Many times I tried to describe my point of view to you, even though it is true that I could not speak very clearly during a time of rented rooms and solitary walks. (I realize that for years the same, almost identical, setting was being repeated around us: empty houses and deserted places.) You refused to accept the most extreme of my arguments—perhaps extending your refusal to include the necessary isolation of our love as well? I claimed that my faith in the French Revolution, my western European education, and my cosmopolitanism, all of these, positioned me against the common bandit; at the same time, however, I was trying, as a revolutionary, to see the causes of an event. Even when it seemed that we lived in different centuries from these brigands or that we spoke a different type of Greek, even then there were moments when my arguments dealt with something very obvious—in similar fashion to my pen, which pulls your form to it in the process of writing characters. I am trying to say that, in certain circumstances, it happened that we fought hand in hand with them. Perhaps I shall have time to write a few words about this further on.

    At that time, the intuition of a woman in love guided you accurately within the space of my silences. To avoid the temptation of asking questions, you used to drag your gaze slowly to the end of a meandering line in the ceiling or to the edge of an Achaian seashore. Once you said quietly, while turning the handle of an umbrella nervously, that the lost future of our love was nothing other than divine wrath. Such naïveté was disturbing to me. Revolution and art demand their price, I yelled back at you. It must have sounded like a falsehood to your ears—to mine as well, I admit—since I was not focusing on your soul but on my own persistence. I asked you if you'd rather not meet again. You thought about it for a moment, a whole moment, and answered no; but you thought about it. I have not forgotten that.

I do not know, Louisa, if the thirty years that have intervened are sufficient for the preparations of a lost revolution to be exposed in every detail, as if it were an event of daily life. Anyway, I shall write to you a few words about our conspiratorial plans since they too, more than anything else, touched the lives of every one of us differently.

Some revolutionary movements of Unliberated Greeks were in the making at that time. The Megáli Idéa had been born and had borne fruit. Personally, I was not as much interested in the revival of the Byzantine Empire—besides, how would it take place?—as in the integration of a modern Greek state, with the prospect of it becoming a member of the future European federation. By "modern" I meant primarily "with a democratic government." I had already published my views on this matter. Besides, I had met privately with Crispi, an old acquaintance from Italy, when he came to Athens to discuss the alliance and related common activities people of different nations were involved in—shortly before he distanced himself from Mazzini's positions in favor of more moderate claims.

Events propelled the trireme of our plans with great speed to all the seas: somewhere the massive form of the Ottoman Empire could be seen half drowned; somewhere nearby the Austro-Prussian and Russian despotisms also were capsizing dangerously. On the other side, the idea of a European federation was upheld by the light—the lighthouses, I ought to say—of a Lamartine, a Michelet, a Quinet, as well as others. This idea continued to attract me even after Othon's dethronement: I should note that the king was not always against the nationalist movements of the Unliberated Greeks, viewing them definitely from his own perspective and in spite of the fact that within his country other movements were being organized every day, closely tied to the nationalist movements, whose aim was his overthrow.

On no occasion, Louisa, was the role of the famous fighters one-dimensional. They did their job, and they did it well. They fought in the revolt of Thessaly and Epeirus: after the Revolution, their armed unregimented squads took part in all uprisings. In no way do I claim that they had the same ideas as we did. They fought with the anticipation of a very concrete exchange, which was usually amnesty for whatever violent acts they had performed in between two revolutionary movements. The movements were almost always unsuccessful, sinking in their own Maremma. Every failure was followed by the acute problem of public safety. So many rebels had arms. It was not easy for them to become members of society again. They camped out near the borders so they could easily take refuge in Ottoman lands. There they worked for some strong politicians, doing exactly what they did in Greek lands when they were on the other side.

The myth of Garibaldi and, at the same time, the rumor about the probability of a campaign in the Balkans to assist the nationalist movements that would break out had inflamed us. Action committees, the so-called *komitata,* did not take long to appear everywhere. I belonged to one of two that were formed in Zakynthos, to the *komitato* of Francisco Domeneginis; the other one was Lombardos's. Both of them were important. We were connected to the Italian *komitata* by way of Cucchi, Garibaldi's aide-de-camp. Domeneginis was also in contact with the general (who had retired to Cambrera) by way of Tour, the former commander of a division of volunteers and the one authorized to make preparations for the uprisings.

I shall not expand further. I shall leave you, Louisa, with the generally correct impression that the *komitata* under discussion were revolutionary organizations with very strict rituals. They were manned by radicals with more or less related objectives, the best of every country—the best, I insist, despite the rivalry and even the pettiness that often sprouted within the organizations.

One more time I avoided the hardships of expeditions and war. It seems that I did not have the slightest inclination for army life. Also, I was not well. More than that, I was a man of letters with international connections, both useful attributes for politics and diplomacy. So I worked in this direction. This did not mean that I was beyond danger; on the contrary, I would say I worked until I was exhausted, without worrying about who supported me, where I slept, or what clothes I wore. I remember only my cape, with which I never parted. However, I had the luxury, since I lived in cities, of being taken care of by experienced doctors, either in Athens or in Patras or elsewhere, if something happened to me. Also, I was not living in continuous unlawfulness.

I admit, Louisa, that many times not even you existed during that period—as if you had not existed at all in my previous life. You were crossed out. Simply so. But, listen to this: shortly after such times, I was looking for the softest mauve and the reddish ink to picture you in my mind in order to see you again, removing you from the gray matter of the rest of the people, rebels or not. I derived the right to remove you from the fact that I was in love. This gave me the most pleasurable guilt, and, many times, it served as something to lean on.

I realize for the umpteenth time that the passion of one in love is turned toward and against his own soul mostly; that in this situation anything real—even the loved one—does not exist beyond the interpretation that the one in love chooses; that, furthermore, nothing changes with the above realization.

Louisa, as time diminishes, a strong wind is driving me steadily toward giving an account of feelings, insisting that they are more important than anything else one has to give an account of—or at least I have to give an account of—and that everything else was paper armor against the onset of even the slightest emotion.

I want to defend myself. I do not know if I shall be able to avoid my disarmament until the end.

Organizing the uprisings properly was difficult. The boots of the apostles had to be worn out, it seemed, the apostles who wandered through the cities and especially through the countryside, using the oddest conspiratorial networks, newly formed organizations, or even the influence of some elders. Their boots were worn out and resoled many times during the course of their endless and utopian, as they turned out to be, wanderings. Despite the optimistic words of the apostles, the people in the villages were afraid after a previous uprising had turned into pure robbery. The leader of the *komitato* to which I am proud to say I belonged would ask Garibaldi, among other things, to raise money from well-to-do countrymen who had businesses in England in order to pay the fighters from Epeirus who would take part in the Revolution well enough so that they would not terrify the local people. Of course, he had the bandits in mind. People had reason to fear them, as I wrote to you, since many rebels were hiding in the mountains after their previous defeat. From there they crossed into Greek territory, looking for a way to reinstate themselves as good citizens—at least that is what they claimed later in their testimonies. They also claimed that they had crossed the borders without knowing that the law deemed them undesirable. Thus, in order to be able to survive, right after crossing the borders, the rebels were forced to unite with the bandits.

This is how things evolved, obliging the public prosecutor in Mesolongi to hear so many stories of Vlach shepherds as he searched for the simple cause that had turned them into bandits, and for the other simple cause that had brought them to the point of committing crimes. Although he made a career out of dealing with crime, I was interested in the cause of crime. I have written all these things to you before, as I have also written to you about the prospect of using the bandits' warfare experience to promote my ideas.

I admit that how close the Megáli Idéa was to ordinary crime disturbed me—I might even say, how close every radical idea is to (allow me) the abuse that its vindication often attracts; I do not exempt even the idea of love. Perhaps that is the reason why I did not go as far as the exaggerations of a well-known young Athenian intellectual at that time who published an essay with the title "Thoughts of a Bandit or Conviction of Society" for the purpose of praising the first and disparaging the second. I had sent it to you, with a letter saying—if I am not mistaken—that lies and truth do not refute each other, especially when both of them are referring simultaneously to the same exaggeration. I did not consider myself young anymore, but that, however, is not the reason that made me disagree with both the assertion of the so-called absolute freedom of the bandits and with the position of the prosecutors toward those whom the first state machinery crushed like wildflowers in its path.

In two years it had crushed them for good, arresting and executing hundreds of them. The philhellenes were concerned about such events, which tarnished the clear blue skies of their Greek ideal. For some time they had the suspicion, which to all intelligent people here was self-evident, that brigandage was simply the peak of an iceberg of political corruption.

When you were staying in your country house in Zakynthos during the harvesting of your family's olive trees, with a native Zakynthian woman as your only companion, you wrote that you were afraid. Your relatives had all moved to Patras or Athens years before. Many had sold their property. An old grandmother in Zakynthos town was measuring out her last days as she counted the passersby in the narrow street. Even though Zakynthos did not yet belong to the Greek nation, you were afraid that you might pay for the sins of those not yet free because the distances were very small. Fear, however, is something more complex, you continued: the more infrequently we met, the more you were concerned about me.

Many times, when I came to Patras, I had to stay in hiding. The fact that I was hiding in my birthplace amused me. I used to say that I was again hiding in my mother's embrace to escape from dragons and wolves. However, she had not lived long enough for me to start hiding from her as I was now hiding from my hometown.

The attic had a window. From it I used to watch the splendid buildings of one of the downtown streets. I knew the owners of most of the homes. On other occasions, I had crossed their thresholds, which now had become prohibited. From up there, the facades of the buildings seemed greener—with tendrils, leaves, and flowers. Step by step, it seemed, the balconies were going down to the sea, obeying the incline of the street. Each building stepped lower down than the one before it, so that there was not one straight line but parts of a straight line joined together, terracelike. I rested my eyes on the arches, which formed wide arcades in front of the shops and moved in harmonious half circles down to the same blue surface. Higher up, the roofs of two- and three-story houses in alternating sequence drew a meandering line in the sky. On the left corner of the street that ran along the waterfront was the big hotel and farther up the pharmacy that belonged to an uncle of mine. Carriages, carts, and passersby added movement to the picture that the city gave to her hidden son, a picture that seemed to be a still life at first glance: ochres, indigo, roof tiles, marbles; in the distance, that mountainous mauve. A colorful and distant embrace.

Easily tempted, I accepted your message to come and find

you in Zakynthos. It was crazy, dangerous, and time consuming, but I did not care. I remembered that a ship was leaving in the evening for its regular route to Zakynthos and Corfu. I notified my organization's contact person to make the necessary preparations. He came back pleased. He was able to secure me a place on an English ship, which was also leaving that evening and following the same route. I would be safer. He brought me the necessary items. Among the papers he brought me I saw the name that I would have during the time that was to follow. Another pseudonym. A merchant of fabrics. As I tried on the eyeglasses, the clothes, and the hat, I found the caution that comes with conspiring once again. I hoped it would work for us.

We arrived just fine. I went through passport inspection quickly. I had to make sure that I escaped the notice of anyone from Domeneginis's *komitato* or from Lombardos's *komitato*, let alone the king's informers. When I arrived at your house, I was still disguised. You laughed and, I think, said that I should boast not only of my revolutionary puritanism but also of the revolt of a man in love.

The sunshine of November—was it November, Louisa?—allowed us to sit the following morning on the veranda, in front of the broad-browed house. At that time the previous day I had been watching the buildings of Patras going down along the straight line of the street, terracelike, until they reached the sea. I should not have become so fragmented. Besides, the times favored the curve. I began to talk to you. For a moment the words scaled the wicker furniture, the pitcher full of myrtle, your wool dress, your hand, your hair, your cheek. One tiny moment. Afterward they disappeared, like drops on dry earth. All around, everything was so quiet—the *alónia* where at harvesttime the currants were spread out to dry, the winepress, the sculptured well, the marble birdbath, the poplars, the olive trees, the cypress trees, the beds of blooming chrysanthemums—that I am wondering if that morning world, if you, Louisa, had understood that we would not see each other again for years. Perhaps never again.

I said that I was tired of giving public farewells to the kindly dead and of giving speeches on national holidays, as if I had in front of me the corpse of our country. The more circumstances headed toward a fateful conflict once again, the more I felt pressured by a need to stand at a distance and, to an equal degree, by a desire to abandon myself to pleasure. Did I want to go into hiding again—as I had hid the day before—in a linen sheet that covered our delayed sleep with leaves of lemon trees?

They were words, and they have been lost. As soon as I returned to my former activities, I pushed the night of love into the darkest blackness in order to have control over my actions. Do not call me cowardly; accommodating and defenseless perhaps.

On the second night I stayed awake at your side. I was to leave before the roosters crowed for a third time, proclaiming that whoever walks in the light of early dawn will surely stumble on his final pangs of conscience. I did not awaken you. A boatman who had been notified waited for me not too far away. He had ferried me from Zakynthos to Killini other times in the past.

It was probably only in my mind that the boatman looked at me strangely while I was engrossed in the sea. It changed slowly from the darkness of the night to the blue of the sky. Alternating imitations: was there a different arena for me? I could not forget that I was born on its imitative waters. For a moment I thought that, just like my peddling ancestors, I was an honest peddler of ideas who pursued a symbolic common profit. In a little while, the morning game the sun plays with the water ended, giving to the sea its usual color. My worldly anxiety lost its morning restlessness. The clear light finally chased away the specter that had kept me company for so long on the boat: waves and wind, their dark love, death at their pleasurable contact. That is how I imagined death, while you,

Louisa, were still turning in my arms. I had to drag my finger over the salt of the gunwale to convince myself that you were not present.

Who should appear in front of me as I walked on the endless seashore later on? The demon of lust. Two whole nights we had yielded our naked flesh and our humbled bones to its indestructible genius. With daring, precision, and grace he had led our bodies to the labyrinth of wanton delight, the delight that, before any god appeared, was identical to the deepest quest for the divine in the forests, the caves, the peaks, the rocks, the springs, the trees—whence nature lends its archaism to bodies that revel in order to praise her, returning to her the echo of the kiss, the laughter, the cry, the stutterings, the whispers—and the benefit of speech, words and oaths of a mortal and necessary peace.

The wise demon walked ahead of me on the sand. For a moment, he bent down on a surface that was wet and smooth because of the waves. He inscribed some characters with his finger, he motioned to me to read them, and he left running. The writing was unknown to me, but I understood, I think, what he meant: that no impression and no curve on the body or the soul of lovers had remained unchanged. A pleasure-giving needle had spread indelible stitches everywhere, unseen by third parties. I, therefore, should have thanked him.

He had reached the front trees of the pine forest that bordered the sand. Before disappearing in its serene greenness, he stood for a minute to see what I would do. I had sat down and was crying, Louisa—looking for your face in my palms, in which I sank my face. I found it and I caressed it—wildly, tenderly, desperately. The demon had not tricked me. Your whole being had been embroidered on me and in me. I had become one with you for always. I loved you.

In a little while I got up and walked till I reached the forest. A villager waited a little farther along with two horses. We started up the hill with the Byzantine fortress at its peak. From the village outside the fortress, I had a way to return quickly to Patras.

I began to have contacts with the *komitata* again in order to coordinate the revolt for the sake of those who had not yet been liberated. Our *komitato* wanted the revolt to be against the monarchy as well. There were many plans of action from many sides. According to ours (I hope I am not violating the rules if I say a few words—after all, why should former conspiracies still torment me?), we had to do the following: to land rebels in Epeirus in order to incite a rebellion in Epeirus and Thessaly and at the same time to depose King Othon in Greece; to form a revolutionary government right away to assist the revolutionaries in the regions that had not yet been liberated, on the one hand, and, on the other, to declare war against the Ottoman Empire. I made the necessary contacts for this plan, or whatever was my portion of the plan, either personally or through correspondence, using a secret code.

As for my lawful life, it continued along the same pattern. Its tone continued to be elegiac in part. The optimistic faith, which I ought to have had with regard to our prospects, often ended in melancholy, as if the latter were better suited to the fate of the land, or at least to my own intuition. Only my detailed prologue to G. A. Naftis's book, *General Principles of Commerce and Its History, as Practiced by the Ancients and the Byzantines,* escaped from this melancholic climate. I also continued being the daring speaker who castigated those responsible for the trials and tribulations of the country. As I was making accusations with such sternness, was I not the very counterpart of a merciless public prosecutor? With these lines, perhaps, I am trying to point out to you, if I have the right to point out anything to you, one more reason that led to your loving the characteristics that he and I had in common, if you have loved both of us, as you maintained. And I put a quick end to this rather pointless parenthesis.

Funeral orations resembling panegyrics and panegyrics resembling funeral orations. One of my last speeches, especially inflammatory, as well as the fact that I was unsuccessful in my attempt to be elected to the Chamber of Deputies—despite the large crowds that gathered to listen to my speeches—made it necessary for me to flee to Italy in order not to be arrested. I shall copy two or three sentences for you from the speech that I gave on the day of the Annunciation in Patras. I always liked this speech:

> ... *Assemblies under the citrus trees in the fair clime of the thyme and the oregano, near the sea, under the blue sky, with a rock as a podium, where, as the cannon of the Aegean and the rifle of the soldier echoed triumphantly from afar, in the same way, from that Homeric podium, echoed the sounds of free speech.* ... *And if Hellas is not revolution, what else can it be, except for a mere geographic expression?* ... *Pain, extreme pain, is a sign of life.* ... *Sweet to the spirit, this thought quivers as the morning star, announcing the coming of spring in the early morning light, smiles erotically to the cool breeze of dawn, to the blossoms of the plains and to the graceful shores.* ...

"And to the graceful shores. ..." I gave a sealed envelope to Hamburger—the industrialist and businessman of Patras, a philhellene of German origin and at the same time a good friend—with the request that it arrive in your hands. I was in his factory at the corner of Maizonos and Zaimi. From there, using his diplomatic privileges as the Prussian consul, he helped me to board an Austrian ship and escape to Italy.

He was happy, he told me seriously, that he would be able to use his diplomatic privileges for this purpose. He did not mention anyone by name, but, as we exchanged glances, we could not avoid an imperceptible smile. An excellent judge of international developments, he accepted the fact that his class should walk along with the virgin goddess of revolutions, as long as on the way the latter did not forget other older and tried types of worship—of Hermes, the god of profit, for instance. Although of German origin and German-speaking, he opposed the Bavarian king, knowing very well that free trade demanded greater political freedom. He had Klaus on his side, who agreed with his views. Along with Hamburger, Klaus was comanager of Fels, Inc., one of the ten most prestigious and ambitious firms in the currant trade of Patras. The Austrian ship by which I would be escaping had been transporting currants and products of their wine industry to Trieste for many years.

I wrote a few words to you on expensive letterhead and sealed the letter in an envelope, both of them having the company name, Fels, Inc., printed on them. Hamburger was going to make sure that you received the letter, a simple enough task, since you had returned to Patras. It seemed to me that the company stationery gave an official character to our separation, but I was too bashful to ask for plain paper.

I would not call the coast that I saw from Hamburger's office window graceful. Not even coastal. A stretched blue braid on the horizon held up the two transparent mountains. The back of the buildings that were used as warehouses by Fels, Inc., hid the road surface of the dock. The national flags of the ships were sticking out over the roofs of the buildings. I definitely knew what was taking place at that moment in front of the warehouses: cases were being weighed on scales, supervisors were overseeing the operations and keeping records, porters and cranes were carrying loaded crates while the tax of 1 percent was paid on the spot. The buzz of the machines did not stop for even a minute, keeping the noises of the dock from reaching us where we were in one of the offices of the firm. It was spring to be sure. However, the hour for which I was waiting seemed independent of seasons and days. My anxiety and, along with it, my inability to do anything other than wait gave everything the slow tempo of perpetuity. I am speaking not only of the view from the window, or of the fact that I was thinking of you, but also of the diplomas and the awards whose whiteness stood out against the darkness of the wallpaper. The green of the wallpaper had not dared to darken like a cypress tree. It was scored by dense vertical lines of ivy. They were gold in color; but it was a different gold than the flame of a candle that turned rose-colored as it traversed your earring, Louisa—and definitely different than the gold of the painting in front of me, where all the evening colors have been condensed in the golden red of the sky. Under it, a gray hill, Karaiskakis's Camp, where young men were resting and talking. A flag, a tent, a dog, two ready horses decked out in full array—I had to hurry.

Few words were spoken—as circumstances demanded: something like, if I am not mistaken, "I have to go," "'When' is unknown, 'if' is unknown," "I do not have time." I think I wrote to you that you should not wait for me. And I signed my real name.

Apparently, I was trembling a little bit. Hamburger offered me a drink. I made a toast to the end of the tyrant and he to my quick return.

After the ship had moved far enough away, I went out on deck to abandon myself to the mien of the Ionian sunset—I mean to say, to the mood of one in love. You had to be set free from the uncertainty of my life. Wish that I could free myself also from the certainty of my feelings. Love demands a continuous future, I thought (and for the first time, it did not bother me that I expressed commonplace views), but also (I'll say it to you here) your volition concerning our affair. Tonight I interpret these as arrogance and as a mistake, but nevertheless as two necessary arrows in the quiver of the god, where good and bad are mixed in liqueurish poisons, since the commonplace is the shadow that accompanies the baby god—if gods have shadows.

Besides, you were married. The danger of being in politics did not bother me, but I was troubled by the thought of endangering my political dream if suddenly our affair became known. It is just as well that you know this, Louisa; I have never touched upon it because of a proper, I believe, modesty, but it troubled me continuously. *"Before me I always saw a past extending"*: here is a favorite statement from the past that captures even my present with clarity. I repeat that, in this enlarged past, not even for a moment was I concerned about the personal price; only about the common price. Anyway, I did not know, or I did not want to know, at what point the one ends and the other begins.

So, then, I assigned the duty of crushing our feelings to the necessary separation. That is how it had to be. I rewrite the suppressive words: the duty of crushing. What naïveté! Let me be harsh. I mock that hour and I mock this one also—as I am writing to you. I mock the fact that you came and stood in front of me; that you smiled bitterly, but so confidently, about your useless, in the long run, triumph; that a ray of light on your earring as you were lying down brought me for a second time in one day to the rose-colored light and to the rose-colored darkness of our naked bodies. You knew me well; and, therefore, you knew that you would possess me as an idea in the most inordinate manner, as you never possessed me as substance.

Your substance I worshiped, Louisa.

I did not write to you during the year and a half that I lived in Italy. Once in a while you must have heard news about me: for instance, that the first half of one of my speeches was printed in the Athenian newspaper *Athena,* which was confiscated in the maelstrom of the uprising at Nauplion. Some words are struggling at the tip of my pen, but they will not avoid being put down finally. Yes, I shall write to you a few words about my activities, which, quite possibly, could remain for many years, if not for always, unknown.

Cucchi, Garibaldi's aide-de-camp, came to Zakynthos, Patras, and Athens in order to talk with the *komitata* and to sort out the role of the court during the impending revolt for liberation. We were all in great confusion. According to the Italian example, Othon's support of the revolt would be useful. However, our *komitato,* at least, fostered the prospect of a simultaneous revolt in Greece against the monarchy, as I have already mentioned. The leader of the other large *komitato,* Lombardos, came to an understanding with Othon; Garibaldi and Victor Emmanuel were in agreement with the Greek plans, under the condition that the king take part. There were repeated deliberations. Finally, Lombardos proposed that Othon's cooperation be accepted but, simultaneously, independent attempts be made to dethrone him if this were necessary. In fact, in a report to the Italian general a little later on, these were his exact words: "If Othon is not a traitor willfully, he is nevertheless a traitor because of his great incompetence and stupidity, which for us is the same."

I am recounting some details of the conspiracy since (I repeat) our lives hinged on their perspicuity or their folly. I agree, mine more than yours—since the drama of conspiracy is never visible to the many immediately afterward; sometimes, for many and various reasons, not even to those putting on the play. I shall finish with generalities: Lombardos's associates, apparently, went to Italy and blamed him for various things, including the fact that the projected revolt had been moved to the courts of Turin and Athens.

I carried a copy of the plans of our *komitato* to Italy. I have to write to you that I interrupted the course of my flight to meet with Domeneginis in Zakynthos and to pick up the plans that I mentioned. I remember the famous musician and composer walking up and down in the room. He kept stopping to look at the green hills outside, as if he were seeing the pages of his music books torn and crumpled. He did not display the familiarity of previous times. There were messages, arguments, and outbursts. He told me not to delay; and he threw me a stern glance, making sure I understood that I should not meet with you during the time—a few hours, for that matter—that I would be in Zakynthos. He probably had heard about our meeting a few months previously, but not that you had returned to Patras. I responded with a direct look while asking myself if that good-bye note had reached you. I wonder whether you had crumpled the stiff paper with the Fels, Inc., letterhead, which attested to the irreversible side of our separation. You must have then straightened it out, perhaps? You must have put it in the cupboard with the rest of the souvenirs, buried seeds of promise? And you must have exorcised the evil with ruins of words that had been previously totally affectionate? And you must have worn the black taffeta dress with the white collar?

Exaggerated guilts perhaps. I sailed away for Italy as soon as possible. The next day the Adriatic was calm; that is the impression of one who has been subdued.

I handed over the plan—more specifically, the latest revisions of the plan—to the Italians. At the same time Lombardos was returning to the palace in Athens. The ambiguity of things made me anxious. I began to doubt the trustworthiness of even the Italian organizations. I was also concerned about the fate of our ideas. What were we intending to accomplish as we forced them to fit into rivalries and mini-causes? Moreover, I was concerned about my fate.

I avoided the company of certain circles and turned toward some old Italian friends. They called themselves royalists at that time. The prospect of what people would say did not stop me because I had been convinced that Victor Emmanuel, contrary to Othon, was reliable and in fact useful at that very critical hour for Italy. I decided to turn publicly against Othon and his participation in the struggle for liberation.

My philippic was given in my beloved Pisa. I had a duty to inform people about the schemes in Athens. I got the opportunity when the students of Pisa organized a splendid banquet to honor me. I began to speak by mentioning the fact that my name was written in the register of graduates of the university with the designations "Patrasso, Giurisprudenza." I had returned; let us add to the innocence of old words the presence of a public orator, revolutionary, perpetual fugitive, former poet, a citizen of the world and one devoted to his country. I left out only one description—the other side of the coin of each of the above qualities, which was indissolubly united with them in the amalgam of my metals: in love. Because I was thinking of you.

The revelation of my political activity, which came from the depths of my being, aroused the students, the professors, and the intellectuals whose presence had honored me at the banquet—citizens especially sensitive to events in other places because they were at a critical moment in their own history. This is the speech I had in mind, Louisa, when I asked you if you had seen the first part of it in the newspaper that was confiscated—unless you avoided everything that had to do with me. Does it matter to you if I write that you are the one I was thinking of even later, when I was translating the speech? Does it matter if I write to you that you possessed me to the extreme, exactly as I had supposed? Or that the Italian wine could not chase you away? No, I do not know of any other separation except for the disappearance of the dead. I turned and kissed your absent lips with the most earthly kiss.

The disappearance—not themselves.

The uprising at Nauplion followed. Its leader, Panos Koronaios, and others who rose up against Othon had no connection to the *komitata*. If I were in Greece then, I would certainly (I think) have been with them; for two whole bloody months, they had risen up in arms. If I had survived, I (along with many others) would have refused the royal amnesty and would have fled to foreign lands. Anyway, Domeneginis and Lombardos asked the Italian members to support the revolutionaries, who had taken refuge in the strong fortresses of Nauplion. As for me, it is about time you learned that, along with Lambros Skaltsas, a descendant of an old and well-known family of bandits in Epeirus who at that time had become a member of the Greek legion of Garibaldi's army, I was recruiting soldiers and sending arms from Ancona to the besieged in the fortresses of Nauplion. My collaboration with the famous bandit went extremely well. However, he spent the following year working for the Bourbons in Italy.

At other times I would not have allowed this collaboration; however, I ask myself to what degree does the success or the failure of a great cause depend on even the smallest fortuitous events, on the smallest gears in the logic of its machinery. Along with this trite but unanswerable question, I shall write down an example to show the spirit that prevailed at that time. During the course of the uprisings at Nauplion, Domeneginis happened to be in Patras. From there he wrote a letter to Cucchi and informed him that he had come across Nikolaos Sahtouris, an old acquaintance and the captain of the *Hydra*, which transported ammunition from Mesolongi to Nauplion for the royalist army. Domeneginis talked to Sahtouris and asked him to take him to Zakynthos. During the course of the trip, Domeneginis disclosed to him a sudden inspiration (which I do not believe was sudden): that Sahtouris wait in Zakynthos till dusk, have three hundred Zakynthians board the ship, give them the weapons that were aboard, and ferry them across the sea to Epeirus to start the uprising for the as yet unliberated; in this way, the Revolution would begin, and the royalists would lose their arms. Sahtouris was enthusiastic and promised to return to Zakynthos to carry out this plan if, in the meantime, he did not do something else on behalf of the revolutionaries in Nauplion.

The letter stopped there; I do not know what happened finally. You judge, Louisa, as you would judge the wind that enters the forest and spreads a fire. If the picture seems simplistic, and most likely it is, keep in mind that the greatest historical events usually attract a simple, again I shall say commonplace, symbolism. Moreover, judge my soul with the same measure that commonplace wisdom uses to exonerate lovers throughout the centuries. My question is different; that is, at what point does the commonplace end so the exceptional can begin? If I do not know how to answer, that is not the only answer.

Alone and bitter, you would not have exonerated me, I suppose. Your own revolt in the area of love had ended so ingloriously; why should you wish for the success of others? Your life would continue near your husband, and he would continue to prosecute the rebels of a civilization many centuries old but already dying. He, too, alone and bitter; I wonder if he knew.

Black taffeta, walks along the pier—there is the sea. Refusal of invitations, complaints about the province—there is the sad woman. In the spring of '62, every once in a while, you moved my letters from the drawer to the balcony that looked out over the Ionian. The written words were decaying and smelled of jasmine. Let their bones at least remain, something tangible—just as the sonata that you had played lingered on the tips of your fingers for hours while you were immersed in your private thoughts. There is the Maremma of love, Louisa.

I knew more or less what you were doing because I kept turning toward the direction where you lived. I was not free to do anything more.

I stayed on in Italy—a second summer. Unbearable months, unbearable bargaining. I was traveling and talking. At the same time, I had a premonition that something definite was on the itinerary in Greece. Dryness and heat. I was not able to relax with either the alternating scenes, the alternating associates, the alternating women, or your steady absence. I remember that every morning I marked the routes of the previous day in a small notebook. Before I was convinced of my great foolishness, I lost it. Everywhere I heard the same words and the same slogans over and over again. The expectancy of the extraordinary event distorted everything. A little later, the sweetness of September and the good turn of events in Italy made my waiting even more torturous—perhaps because I knew that the end would have many facets: a hateful monarchy would come to an end; my asylum in the neighboring country would come to an end. You lived always in the homeland. Your taffeta darkened the perspiration in my palms, and the future of the land darkened the blood in my heart.

I did not return right away after Othon's dethronement. I waited a few weeks, until things settled down—things and that inspired madness that overtook me.

A welcome "that no one else was fortunate to have in Greece"—words of the press, which you may have read. The exceptional welcome was impressed on my mind like an honorary medal of the city, a medal the city would ask me to return relatively soon; but it would no longer be able either to wrest it away from me or to cancel the hour of its offering.

I was standing on deck while the ship cast anchor out in the open sea. The light November rain did not prevent the songs of the crowd on the dock from reaching the deck of the ship. In a little while, as the boat approached the marble pier, I saw the people who had swarmed the pier, the customhouse square, the streets in front of the warehouses, and the nearby roads. Most of them had stopped at the square in front of the customhouse, which was built over the drained marshland. Again I could not avoid the word "Maremma." Frightened, I turned my attention to the simple patriotism of the antiroyalist songs. One of them was heard more than the others. I had written the words.

Wreaths and flowers on the calm waters. I began to distinguish faces on land. All the citizens in a celebratory illusion of equality, the only feasible one perhaps. The band started playing; it seemed that the friends took a step forward. Shortly I was kissing them.

The light rain had stopped. The open carriage went up the main street slowly. The people all around continued singing and tossing flowers. It was still light out, but a group of young men honored me by holding lighted candles and accompanying the carriage, which soon turned to the street your home was on. My Lord and my God, I had forgotten you!

The front door was closed. I thought with relief that at this time of the year you might be in Zakynthos for the olive harvest. Suddenly I saw the shutters of the balcony door open. The imperceptible movement of the curtain left me no doubt. You were standing there. You did not share in the celebration.

All of a sudden, whatever I remembered of you flashed in front of me. Your black taffeta rustled "like a wind that enters the forest and spreads the fire." It rustled as it fell on the floor and left you so bare.

29 december 1888
on the train

Louisa, I am writing to you on the train as I am traveling to Athens. The ride on the train is shorter than the sea voyage. Besides, I did not want to see Patras again from the sea. I am afraid, however, that I am losing a sense of time by writing to you. I must keep track of time, I must.

In Athens I shall stay two days and shall not visit anyone. I reckon I shall take the steamship that serves the Piraeus-Ermoupolis line on New Year's Eve. I hope it will not be crowded. Who would be traveling on such a day unless it were absolutely necessary? Besides, how many will remember that a hundred years have gone by since the outbreak of the greatest revolution? Among the very few, how many are going to keep silent for a moment, while French champagne bottles pop at New Year's parties?

Louisa, I am asking you to excuse the totally fragmentary nature of whatever I write to you from this point on. In about two and a half days, I have to cover twenty-five years—a somewhat telegraphic system of writing would be very helpful. Besides, my life during this period is more or less known, while other years—the undocumented life?—take much space in narrations that come from deep within; that may be one reason why they are undocumented. I would like to add that the last twenty-five years, although productive, do not excite me with the same degree of interest; but it is possible, too, that I simply misjudged the amount of time that I had available and the number of things that I wanted to write to you about. Any other explanation is also possible. So, some thoughts, some feelings, some excerpts. That is enough.

Besides, nothing can hold on to the promise of its birth because of a more or less secret aversion to its materiality (and to the future of its materiality), which is to be destroyed.

In the meantime, it is possible for anything to happen, being indifferent to our fixed symbolisms and to the passion of our personal entanglement.

Was abandoning ourselves equally to the truth and to the fantasy of being in love worthwhile—so there would be no sign left of the names of the lovers?

The inspector asked for my ticket and gave it back with a blank look. I did not avoid giving him an archangelic smile: one more pointless symbolic act. Be it so. Let me hold on to the privilege of my melancholic rhetoric. I shall try not to sleep, even though the rhythm of the train—why not, the rhetoric of the machines—is dangerously lulling, and my hand is not steady on the paper. I do not foresee any excerpts of life—only the notes of a traveler.

The last few days and nights I have been writing to you constantly. However, I must confess to you one lone exception.

Yesterday, 28 December, when I finished with these pages very late, I wrote two different notes. I shall explain: first of all, I was afraid that perhaps Dante's two half lines would not be enough as the epigraph of my work, which Vasilis is getting ready to publish; and, second, who would understand what I mean by them? I thought about it again (I have already written to you that this tormented me) and finally decided to dedicate my work *"to the first of the modern Greek generations, which time would show that, in word and in deed, it distinguished itself."*

I wrote it on a piece of paper, and in the morning, before boarding the train, I mailed it to the printing shop with the request that it be printed exactly above the Dantean half lines. I do not mean to connect the "distinguished generation," if it will ever come to be, to my own paternal melancholy. I am sixty-seven years old, and life has avenged me enough for the violence that I exercised over my feelings when I was younger. Whether it was a matter of necessity or not does not always count.

I felt something like panic when faced with the question of who will attend to whatever is already arranged.

I felt the need for tenderness. What an irony!

I pick up the yarn again. May you be the only one to know, Louisa, that a second note was drawn up and written in Patras yesterday, even though I shall mail it from Athens. I pretended, however, that I wrote it in Athens by placing "Athens" in big letters next to the date. Anyway, they do not know if I was in Patras all day yesterday, and I have time until they receive both the first and the second note. I want my peace, which is why I made this maneuver.

I wrote and rewrote the second note. I have not sealed the final version yet. I shall copy it and entrust it to you so that, if you ever see it in print, you can compare its authenticity. I requested that it be on a page by itself, as follows:

To my friends,
Vasilios G. Kalliontzis (from Patras, living),
Asimakis Asimakaros (from Patras, deceased),
Dem. Georgiadis (from Mani, deceased),
Spiros Dousmanis (from Corfu, deceased).

I certainly had, and I have still, many other friends who will remember me even after death and will continue my patriotic work with sincerity.

But I wish your names to remain within my book, associated with my name by subsequent generations because you, especially, supported me and encouraged me spiritually and materially, and you loved me with dedication and sacrifice throughout your life.

Athens, 28 December 1888

I signed it. I did not mention anything regarding the poems and the theatrical works; they are not, nor were they ever, an end beyond patriotism.

30 december 1888
athens

I am continuing from Athens, Louisa. I am staying at a hotel. Yesterday I fell asleep on the train. It got dark so early. I had my friends on my mind constantly, the ones I thanked in the note that I wrote—faces floating outside the window: on lemon trees full of fruit and on bare vineyards; on a deep sea, filled with its own white figures; on a rowboat pulled out on the pebbles; on pale mountainsides hanging over candlesticks of cypress trees and clusters of pines. Remember their names.

I wonder who among the friends had won immortality? And by what means? The aspirations of a dying romanticism?

The immortality of a friend is based on lost time shared: communicants of an immaculate wine or a wine-drinking sea?

One more thing: friendship has a two-way relationship with death in exactly the same way as love does.

So I had closed my eyes. Inside my eyelids, the blue, green, and mauve colors of the evening continued to shine. I did not want my friends to be in the dark.

This month deepens the colors to a point of anguish.

I dreamed of the death of your husband.

When he was killed, people said those responsible must have been bandits, from among those who knocked about the country between the dethronement of one king and the arrival of the next. His corpse was found in a boat that had been set adrift, which moored at a seashore in the Gulf of Patras. He had been killed with a bullet in the back. There was no end to this case. People said that he had received threats because attempts were made at that time to have the bandits put down their arms in exchange for amnesty, since everyone was afraid of traveling anywhere because of them—even after George's arrival. Moreover, they themselves did not have another way of putting the past behind them and starting anew. But he continued to stand firm. . . . However, something else was heard also—that they were not bandits but a small gang of smugglers, whom he had tracked down and was preparing to prosecute.

I happened to be in Patras as a deputy of the district of Achaia after my huge victory in the elections of '65. I had more votes than even Benizelos Roufos, with whose party I ran for office. Some newspapers, forced to support the candidacy of a citizen who was not a landowner, mentioned that my ailments did not allow me to work and that I had relinquished my inheritance by deed—for the purpose of concluding that I stood out for my patriotism, my knowledge, and my unselfishness. There were plenty of accusations, however, of the following type: conceited, impostor, idiosyncratic, Don Quixote. I am not sure if all these characterizations were made during those elections or on other occasions.

What made me write to you about both praise and reproach? Anyway, I happened to be in Patras when the murder took place. I realized that we had not seen each other since I had returned from Italy. I want to make this clear: I did not try to meet you. I lived mostly in Athens, devoted to politics. I know that is not enough, but such were the times then, and many of us subscribed to this way of thinking. Yes, I had some other relationships. Vanity, or what we call life? I keep those years illuminated; even though at times their light hid a—what can I call it?—a familiar darkness. In Patras I was a man with old history—every type of history. I do not rule out that for this reason I preferred Athens—when I was around forty-five.

The news of the murder pulled you out of the Maremma of forgetfulness, where I had pushed you with a light stroke of the hand. I do not deny that I was shaken, as if a punishing angel had hit me hard with his whip. Or perhaps that wise demon? I dug my nails in my palms so I would not yell out your name, so I would not rush straight to your house. In a little while I calmed down; and then I was embarrassed because my passion had preceded the sadness due to the dead person. Besides, I owed it to the friend of my childhood and my student life to mourn him. I shall not shy away from writing that I owed it to the companion of your life also. Did he make a simple and fateful mistake of taking the opposite path than the one I took, or did I, perhaps, make a mistake by taking the opposite path than the one he took? For the umpteenth time I asked myself why we loved the same woman, and, especially, why we tolerated each other in this dangerous situation. I cannot find an answer. Nor am I certain whether the love of one man resembles the love of another. Nevertheless, I got very upset by the fact that they laid an ambush for him. From that time on, I would be completely against this customary justice, which, lacking the courage of a face-to-face confrontation, pierced the flesh of centuries in the treacherous manner of an inherited ailment. Anyway, so to finish, at that time there was a recurrence of what had been happening steadily. Along with the most enlightened, the most upright volunteers, a few bandits boarded the ship for Crete, which was in the midst of a revolutionary uprising. Many people did not react against the composition of this expedition, perhaps because they thought it would be good to rid the place of both the former and the latter. As for me, this proved to me once more that no society is homogeneous with respect to its makeup and its synchroneity. On the other hand, is this not one of its driving forces?

I came to the church and stood a few meters away from you. Was it marble or copper behind the transparency of mourning black? I could not bear to see you this way, and I forced my gaze to turn elsewhere, while I abandoned myself to the drug of incense and verses. Calmed, I came up to you to greet you. Neither marble nor copper. Your face had the vagueness of souls.

I left immediately for Athens.

The vagueness of souls: listen to the dream I had on the train yesterday.

My friends, one of them living and three deceased (whose names I wrote for you and asked you to remember them), and I were on the prowl for the prosecutor. It was very dark all around, and the five of us were invisible in the dirty black *foustaneles* and the dark capes. Since I was first on the dock, I ordered a plain soldier to fire at our pursuer and grant him death without torture. We heard the bullet and the groan. We dragged him to the sea and threw him in a shallow boat, like those in the lagoon or in the Maremma. We let it loose. Then we took off for the nearest hideout. We walked all night with light and quick footsteps, as bandits walk. We arrived. We had nothing to divide; the liquidation had no connection to money. We fell asleep at daybreak without eating. No one objected that I was thinking of you, his wife. Women had no place in our lives, neither in the life we lived nor in the life we foresaw on the shoulder blades of sheep.

My hotel is in the district of Neapolis. Outside the sun is shining. I am wondering whether, annoyed by the dream I had yesterday, you threw away my manuscripts. I shall not take the dream back.

I was happy that I had been elected deputy at the start of a new epoch, as we believed. As history writes its own fiction with its symmetrical letters, it allows once in a while the asymmetry of such false illusions.

To proposals regarding new taxation measures, I counterproposed the need for the nation to exploit the mines in Lavrio. I gave warning about the revolt in Crete before it broke out, maintaining that we should not rely on diplomacy but only on ourselves.

Memorable orations in the Chamber of Deputies: "*Woe to those who do not see. . . .*" Certainly they did not want to see.

Memorable funeral orations, since the new epoch demanded a different type of oratory—I would not call it completely opposite to that of the anti-Othon period. On the first pages you are holding, there is the following sentence from the speech I gave at the memorial service for the military doctor who had volunteered to go to Crete, Ioannis Vasiliou: "*Our century is reaching its end; it is approaching its denouement.*" I began with a memory: in 1848, about twenty years earlier, when the people of Europe undertook the hymn of their future, I happened to be in the ruins of Asine, in Portolo, with friends. We were welcomed by Cretan refugees who had fled there after an unsuccessful uprising on their island in '21. "*One of them, in a corner of that pleasant desert, was playing the lyre, but so sadly. . . .*" Even now, as I write to you, Louisa, I hear its lament, as I heard it then also, in the church, accompanying my words for the doctor, the son of a well-known fighter, one who had taken part in all the liberating movements, without ever making a distinction between his profession and his country. "*The person who dies in such holy battles drinks instantly all infinity . . . as if it were one drop. . . . Such deaths do not call for mourning clothes but for white. . . .*"

White—I looked around me at the dark overcoats. I looked for the unblemished color on faces lit by candles. In the first row all were well known, most of us belonging to the Central Committee in support of the Cretans, with my old friend, Markos Renieris, as president and the benefactor Antonios Kampanis Papadakis as treasurer. Looking at their faces I had the feeling—why, however?—that shortly the Revolution, "*the material struggle for the sake of an idea,*" would change its character radically. In any case, the change would have to do with the theatrical element, since it never takes place only for the idea that it invokes and presents at the forefront. So the time had arrived when the palace, faced with the scene of revolution, would change its method in order to express the substance and the imagination of a different present? I wonder what this drama would gain from its modernistic scenic effects.

Blood takes its time, but it always takes revenge. From the time of deposit until the time of cashing in, an amount is withheld—to keep the majority in fear.

An idea does not have flesh, but it implies the death of the flesh or, worse yet, its degradation in torture chambers.

Only in love is flesh tender, but even with this ploy flesh cannot avoid its decay.

I started to correspond with Quinet again. I told him that at one time I had a great deal of property but that now I was a poor man. I could not live in Greece from my publications alone. I wanted to carry out a plan of action to assist the suffering revolutionaries on Crete. I explained it to him and pointed out that it required money. Would he be able to send me some of the money that was raised in Europe for such purposes? Could he not hear the death woes—certainly not the lyre—of those brave men? Some captains would not give up. . . .

I knew that this revolution also was approaching a denouement without catharsis. Was it an extreme imitation of history or simply the timely conclusion of my century? I did not write to him my sad thoughts, which, in any case, did not allow me to be careless.

In a previous letter I had mentioned to him that the Parthenon was sighing, that new martyrs are being born every day, that old lady Europe laughs like Satan himself and makes fun of us; in her dealings, she favors the Ottoman. As for our politicians, they are men without morals and capabilities. If he would only raise his voice, before the expected end.

It was too late. In six months everything was finished.

You began to write to me from Zakynthos, where you had gone for an extended period of mourning. Infrequently, true; but my letters were even more infrequent. You had asked me for a copy of my only photograph, and I sent it to you. You answered that you were startled by its likeness to me. It seemed like treachery, as if I were betraying myself retroactively to my pursuers of any given time. But when the first impression had passed, you were able to trace love's terrain. Later on you asked me if I continued to write poems.

No, I had not written poems for a long time.

Your words: a leaf that led me to your tree. I leaned on the shade to hear its whisper whole.

Would we meet again? Neither one of us could decide to take the first step. Maturity was the most embarrassing stage of our life.

You thought of me. This was also a type of mourning. However, you did not believe in resurrections from the dead. This was your way of reconciling with fate. You called fate something irrevocable, heavy and pleasurable. Mourning and reconciliation then.

You also wrote that you were growing older, sacrificing the contours of your form drop by drop to the amorphous god of time. However, will the gift of a meditative sensibility suffice for the loss of form? Whatever does not have a shape is ugly. You would never stand in front of that machine in order to send me the photograph that I had requested.

Would you have stood in front of me, the one who knew you as spirit?

I shall write down some more details about myself, since at that time I became involved in other activities besides those that had to do with being a deputy.

A few years before the Paris Commune, the International Convention of Peace and Freedom convened in Lausanne. I was a member, but financial reasons prevented me from going. I composed my speech directly in French, and I sent it to the convention. Later on it was published in Greek, at the expenditure of friends, as always. Allow me once again to copy two or three lines from this speech, which I consider the quintessence of my mature years and of an epoch:

> *Revolution is the diverse illumination of an idea, the partnership of thoughts and of people. . . .*
> *Revolution is Jesus preaching to the people and, simultaneously, reviling those who oppress the people.*
> *And, moreover, it is Heracles setting Prometheus free. . . .*
> *Revolution is the law of progress.*
> *And progress does not take place except by way of movement. . . .*

I signed it "Your brother from Greece" and added my real name and the title "former deputy." Unfortunate wanderings guided my speech to Lausanne after the convention ended. Quite a few excerpts from this extensive text were published in a newspaper there.

The sentence "Revolution is the law of progress" soon would become the epigraph of the only issue of a newspaper that the People's Democratic Union published in Patras, which was confiscated right away, while the members of the union were taken into custody. My name never appeared among the names of the twelve founders, all of whom—most of them intellectuals—were people from my close circle of friends. However, I co-signed the documents for the founding of the Athenian organization Rigas, of which I am proud to have been a member, along with the staunchest individuals of that time; I mention only Panayiotis Panas and Roccos Hoidas.

Louisa, it is not worth tiring you with the disagreements, the ambitions, and the evasions—nor with the new prosecutions, arrests, and court trials that had broken out in the large cities. Besides, these are well known. I note only that the above-mentioned organizations had some common positions, naturally up to a point, which they published in their newspapers. For instance: ignorance and poverty were the greatest wounds of our people; social misery sprang from them; liberation from them was the aim of each one of us, if one wanted to work for the country, because liberation from them would bring equality with regard to both rights and responsibilities, and, close behind, freedom to the unliberated brothers; people, in order to be liberated, have to rise up by themselves; their freedom will always depend on the degree of their emancipation, because man has been created free and master of himself. . . .

I had dinner brought to my room. As I was eating, I raised my eyes—for the first time in so many hours—and looked outside. It is too bad that I do not have time; I would like to go for a walk.

I am thinking of the statement "Revolution is the law of progress" once again. It is based equally on revolution's right to be always present and on the realization of its future strength. With these six words the departing romanticism holds the childish hand of realism, which the latter allows trustingly, for the time being.

I see my own hands again as I write. They give me the impression that everything is gone, having left with the greatest possible speed, the speed of a steam engine, and, at the same time, the impression that I am viewing my life from the distance of a reader. But the steam engine will not stop at the hotel room. It will continue its frenzied night itinerary.

Night upon night of sleeplessness—thinking and rethinking that perhaps every formulation for a revolution ought to include the prospect of its deviation. Being very young—as all of us were then—I had overlooked the aftermath of the French Revolution in order to be nourished by its driving sense of justice. To what degree was I correct? The answer obviously is based on what is correct. Woe, who will be the judge of that?

Behold the Maremma once again.

You stayed in Zakynthos for years, giving your life a different meaning after your mourning. I never found out exactly what meaning. You complained that I seldom wrote to you. You heard about me, however, from the press and from acquaintances. You heard, for instance, that an association was formed in Patras under the leadership of Asimakis Asimakaros and Vasilis Kalliontzis for the sake of supporting one more attempt on my part to be elected deputy; that Asimakis spoke about me at a gathering and said that for twenty years I held the flag of the struggle high, which was consistent with my principles, that I was always on the alert, tireless, indomitable, "preferring to sacrifice youth, property, vanity, and a comfortable way of life, and even to be mocked, rather than to contribute to the destruction of the country . . . even though he could have shared any shred of authority better than thousands of others, and he could have attended to selfish interests, pursuing riches and vain honors"; that, after demonstrating in the city holding lighted candles, all those gathered walked to my house, and I thanked them from the balcony before going down so we could all march to Kapodistrias Square together, where I gave a speech. For some reason I referred to this famous oration, entitled "Awakening," on these pages (near the beginning, I think) and to the fact that I was not elected. Actually, I finished fourth runner-up. The echo of the Paris Commune of a few months earlier still disturbed, it appears, the lull of all who had property, vanity, a comfortable life, and an inviolate name—the lull of most.

You wrote how much you had been moved by the articles

about me in the *Greek Revolution*. The same newspaper announced the publication of my complete literary and political works, an attempt that fell through. It is just as well. Now I can share what I have done with my devoted friends. Does it matter which friend is still living and which is dead?

The premiere of my first dramatic work, *John Milton,* was to take place in the Apollo Theater in Patras, which had been completed two years previously. The hand of Ernest Chiller had drawn the plans, and the wishes and money of both foreigners and natives had contributed to bring about the completion of the magnificent building. *John Milton* had been published by the Phoenix in March, even though the performances were to start in November. I had sent you the book a little before the premiere. In a brief prologue I remember that I wrote, among other things, the following:

> *Certainly the English nation at that time represented a spectacle of moral collapse, both internally and externally, after an especially magnificent uprising and a great revolution, during which democracy was declared, of which Cromwell was its president and Milton its minister. . . . Only one great personality sheds a beautiful and comforting light on this miserable period of the English nation: John Milton, already blind, persecuted, threatened, and abused. . . . In writing the play you hold in your hand, we were motivated, as always, by the idea of doing our duty to our country. . . .*

I was referring indirectly to the reign of King George, but not exclusively to it.

You promised to watch the premiere from your box at the theater. However, you could not reconcile yourself (that is what you wrote, or was it "become accustomed," perhaps?) to the idea of our meeting. I belonged to you in the incomplete manner of a man given elsewhere. If we were to meet, we would keep the distance imposed by something sacred. Anyway, how can one be present at the lost paradise of his own love? You wrote that a parallel teaching could refer to the two of us.

Such thoughts tormented you, but you promised to come, both for the importance the staging of my first dramatic work had for me and for the pleasure promised by incomplete meetings—and you did not fail to point out right away that in our desire for the incomplete is concealed our bitterness for the cancellation of the whole. If there is such a whole.

With these words you foretold the cancellation of the premiere: as I read your letter on the eve of the premiere, stupid me, I did not fathom the meaning behind the lines of writing. Louisa, you, who have been the reason for my material substance and for the substance of my meditation, tell me at last if it was a matter of fate or your own witchery that we did not meet that evening. You, who had taught freedom the meaning of obligation—and to the orator you had taught the inexpressible—were neither in the theater nor out on the square, where people had gathered to protest the sudden cancellation of the performance. Word spread that the president of the theater committee had imposed censorship—as was his right. You did not see the gendarmerie on horseback in the street in front of the wide staircase of the entrance, nor did you hear the pronounced disavowals of the crowd that was becoming dense in the square. We came close to having incidents.

That is how this unexpected first event ended. I found myself sitting alone in one of the crimson seats of the theater. Some of the 150 wicks of the chandelier were still lit. The set that had been prepared behind the screen could not be seen. On the canvas of the screen I saw the painted waterfront of Patras, the sea, the mountains across, and a ship with open sails heading out. Gold and white garlands of plaster and the folds of the open crimson curtain bordered the prison of the pictured landscape. Up high, at the center of the curtain, loomed the emblem of the kingdom of Greece, golden, on blue cloth. Higher still, in the middle of a carved metope and exactly over the two men with the shield, a big clock held by two lovers pointed to eight o'clock.

Exactly eight.

Later you had made excuses for your absence. You certainly had not foreseen the imposition of censorship and the cancellation of the performance. You had found out about this from the newspaper, and you were disturbed. You did not come for the following simple (as you characterized it) reason: when you finished reading *John Milton* a few days before it was to be staged, you doubted whether I had ever loved you even for a moment, since I had in my mind such women as Milton's daughter—impervious, faithful to the dreams of her loved one, courageous when confronting the enemy and her death. You conveyed in your letter part of my dramatized feelings:

> *As the drowning man trusts in divine providence, as the child in the mother's smile, as the just man trusts the judgment of subsequent generations, I trusted in you. . . . Love was a flame, through which the divine in my soul was perpetually rekindled! . . . Your love made my love toward my country divine, it infused a spirit of creation in my soul, it inflamed my feeling toward everything true, great, and illustrious in the world. . . . Virtue, heroism, compassion, and the lofty feeling of sacrifice, by way of your love, took on in my soul the brightness of an archangelic sword!*

You did not want to come.

In my last (explanatory) letter, I informed you that Milton's three, hardly affectionate, daughters had been condensed to one in my play. Despite information to the contrary, the oldest daughter, Anna, had been transformed into my very beautiful and courageous heroine. I had followed closely the demands of my melodrama, in which good and evil were separated in a very simple—and for this reason very popular—manner. Louisa, you also knew the conventions of this type well. What was the matter?

My life was neither a life of writing nor a life of theatrical performances, despite all that ruled over it and weighed it down. Behold the most tangible proof: the things that I have written to you in the pages you are now holding. Otherwise, I would have confined myself, if there were nothing else, to my two theatrical works. I could have let you remember me thus.

That letter was mean. I was not so much bothered by your refusal to come as much as by the ease you displayed in finding such reasons behind which to hide. You were hypocritical, and you acted as if this was not pure theater but your life.

What were the two of us afraid of after all?

I saw *John Milton* on the stage eight years later, specifically, in the summer when the actor Lekatsas came to Patras to present Shakespearean drama. One evening he ventured to present *John Milton*. I was a deputy again, independent this time. I entered the theater accompanied only by my friends. I could not stand being alone; I was getting old. The play was unsuccessful. My appearance was mentioned (with ironic remarks) in a local newspaper. Lekatsas, whom Vlassis Gabrielidis, perhaps the most important journalist in the country, considered the best among his peers, spent whatever money he had left to make sure all the ladies of his troupe had tickets for the steamship. The rest started off with him on foot for Athens. It took them nine days to arrive.

The years passed. They resembled one another, I think. I lived most of the time in Athens, but I often visited the district that had elected me (let me refer to it thus at least once)—Patras.

Welcoming crowds at the waterfront, addresses, catapulting speeches, triumphs, and slanders. I have not forgotten all the things that I should have forgotten.

I was always in a hurry; tired; after a certain point in time, aged.

I ask myself if I have written to you already the things that I wanted to write to you.

But with what word does life end?

The light of a perennial dawn and the light of a private sunset: the spark of their contact.

Would we perhaps have been able to stand the spark of our meeting?

Suddenly—again I am counting by decades—I received the most strange letter, your last letter. You were always frightened of the silence regarding the murder of your husband. I wished we had stayed pure and sinless as on the eve of our first meeting, even though there never was a paradise that was not lost.

If you only raised the mask of a graceful seashore just a little bit, the wave would become oceanic. There you made the decision to be alone; and you leaned on the pebbles, forgetting the tide. The one who came to save you was the man you had married, pale, condemned to remember. You raved in his arms with the words of a woman who had been alone for years. In between two kisses, his face had become mine. I was pale also, condemned to remember.

In the morning you sat down right away to write to me.

Louisa, what is truth in the rhetoric of a letter? I mean to say, what is truth in the rhetoric of a dream?

I do not ask for the sake of an answer.

The only one to whom I had spoken about you was Asimakis, the dearest of my friends. Like a king who had been caught in the most plebeian foolishness, I had intended for him to continue my work.

During the last few years he looked after me. And he listened to me.

31 december 1888
athens, noon

Louisa, it is now noon. The sun keeps shining in Athens. I told the hotel owner to call for a coach. It was not easy because of the holidays. Crossing Aiolou Street and Monastiraki to get to the café that I used to frequent was even harder. Luckily, my table near the window was unoccupied. Many times I had counted the eight windowpanes. In the distance was the Acropolis, beautifully sunlit. The same sun rewarded my walk by leaving a coin near the edge of my writing paper. I accepted it. How much will the boatman ask for? Your profile was engraved on the one side. I did not turn it over. I was not interested. The sun moved it slowly from the paper to the marble tabletop. Then it disappeared.

My second dramatic work, *Nero in Corinth,* which was my first successful piece of writing, was staged by Vasiliadis ten years ago in the month of May in Patras. In August of the same year it was presented here in Athens by the Tavoularis brothers' troupe, the Menander. It was published by the Mentoros Printing Press. Katsimpalis funded its publication.

I do not have time to write any more either about this work or the performances. I doubt that you would be interested. I shall mention only that Emmanuel Roidis praised it, and that, as I was celebrating the success of *Nero* with friends and cool retsina, I sensed you were afraid of me as a victor, as a public figure, as presence—or perhaps I am again mistaken? I think Asimakis, sitting next to me, also saw your hand clouding the wine, pouring in the right amount of melancholy for such a delayed victory. I am speaking about the success of *Nero*.

You—the friend of an old reflection, the friend of our youthful images. In a way you were not on a very different course than the writer of dramatic works. I idealized young couples soon to be married—on virgin white, while we fell in love on the whiter-still lightning of blackness.

You were afraid, I suppose, of the immortality that I would win, I, the equally mortal—an immortality which would have no relation to our love. You were never comfortable with the fact that a man's relationship with death is a completely different story than the relationship between a woman and death.

Romanticism is ending.
And a way of falling in love is also ending.
But are they ending?

Elected deputy once more, I gave speeches attacking the sad state of the economy and the army, of education and manufacturing; I even questioned the legitimacy of the elections. Practically none of the pronouncements of the new government had been carried out; practically none of those I had heard from the prime minister himself when he visited Patras on Christmas, just a few days after his victory—and I heard them with difficulty, mixed in with the cheers of the crowd that filled the streets and later the theater, where Trikoupis had gone to watch *Lucia de Lammermoor* with Ciaramonte singing soprano. While the prime minister addressed the people in a greeting from the central box, the orchestra kept playing the national anthem. Later, I could not hear any pronouncements at all among the noise of the fireworks and the applause that accompanied him to the waterfront after the performance. A lighted ship with engines running was waiting to take him on the urgent night journeys where politicians go—journeys usually full of nightmares.

Exactly eight years ago I gave a speech in Athens, entitled "Regarding the Neighboring Provinces of Epeirus and Thessaly," following the directive of the National Coalition. Rigas's organization, as I mentioned to you earlier, had already been dismantled. Anyway, it was nothing more than the legal Greek version of a broader, longer-lasting, and secret society, the Eastern Democratic Federation. This society, for fifteen whole years during the century that was ending for me, carried the vision of Pheraios, broadening it with Mazzini's ideas as well as with some of the more recent socialist ideas. Times and events allowed it to speak for a Balkan federation from the Alps and the Carpathian Mountains to Crete and Cyprus, but, as was the case with Rigas, it was silenced by the first independent Balkan states that had just been created. That is when Thessaly was ceded to Greece, and, as a representative of the very recently organized National Coalition, I spoke to the troops who had been drafted to march on to Thessaly in two days. My speech was published with the title "Liberated Greece Has to Enforce the Decision of the Berlin Conference on Its Own." I recall a few points:

> . . . *The greatest ideal for you should be Greek national identity, independent and free but complete, for national identity forges great men, upstanding characters, and distinct forms of civilization and of the arts when there is self-sufficiency, when there is diversity, but diversity in unity. One national identity, complete and self-sufficient, is also one of Plato's sublime ideas, one of Aristotle's entelechies, one lofty personality, a cherubic liturgy.* . . .
> *From the peaks of Olympus extend your hands toward the other peoples of the East, even toward the Turks, because they too have the capacity for progress and perfection.*
> *Tell the Romanians, the Serbs, and the Montenegrans that*

their interests lie in an alliance with us so that both they and we can throw off once and for all the yoke of our old oppressor. . . . They are capable of becoming the power of the land, and we, the power of the sea; and then we will be invincible. . . .Then the Bulgarians too will be forced to stay within their own borders, living and progressing along with all of us, and no ambitious man will be able to incite them in the future. . . . Tell the Albanians, our fellow brothers who are separated from us, that their only salvation is their cooperation and union with us Greeks. . . .

Then one Eastern Federation. . . . Then the peace of the East will spring forward. . . .

Then, Louisa.

Disparaging remarks against me started to appear a long time ago, but at that particular time they became more intense. They were based primarily on my refusal to go along with the most powerful parties. The isolation of my life, my indifference toward money, and the rest of my ideas certainly were provocation enough. Newspapers that used to support me steadfastly turned against me at some point, as if they had for years awaited an opportunity to deal me this blow. However, I still had large audiences when I spoke in assembly rooms and city squares. I think I was the first one at that time to speak up in the Vouli, the Chamber of Deputies, and to recommend the establishment of a bank of agriculture and real estate. No one took special notice; besides, these were the proposals of a dreamer.

One day I saw the following statement in the press in Patras: "Who are you? The few adolescents who were following you till now have gone away from you forever. You have only a few mindless democrats left." I also saw myself caricatured in the Athenian publication *Asmodaios*, reprimanding nature for the earthquakes. At the same time, Patras used to welcome me as its eminent deputy. My speeches were published immediately after they were given. They were "eloquent" and I was a "popular and practical man."

Carnival: February or March during the last few years; all of Patras once again sacrificing to the graceful wine god commemorated at that time of the year. The time when masquerading gave individuals the opportunity to clear every type of account, when even stabbings were not ruled out, was not far off. I was against such doings without denying the need for an abstract, a symbolic, drop of blood in these very ancient celebrations. For obvious reasons, I was one of the dancing partners for waltzes, away from the danger and spectacle of the streets—until at some point I stopped frequenting the beautiful, I confess, dances, scandalized by the waste, and not only that, by the purchases of exotic wings, golden fabrics, silver masks: a blind, superficial, uniform good life, indifferent even to good theater. The people celebrating in the streets had more spirit.

On the last Sunday of the carnival I was standing among the dignitaries of the city on the balcony of the Apollo Theater. We were looking at the hullabaloo below and discussing the construction of the harbor, the new taxes, and the bankruptcies while we waited for the parade of floats to begin. Suddenly, out of the corner of my eye, I saw myself near the upper fountain of the square. Let me be more precise: I saw the naked man with the flute, Eros at his feet, the four lions of the large basin, and, about a meter in front of them, myself, lifelike, imitating my walk. The crowd gathered all around and began to laugh as my caricature took off a top hat and bowed. The impersonator had not forgotten to protect himself from the cold by a cape, similar to the one I was wearing on the balcony, and to protect his identity with a black mask.

My eyes were transfixed on my caricature; in contrast, my experienced tongue controlled its surprise. As for those with whom I was conversing, some of them pretended that they paid no attention and others began to laugh, supposedly secretly. I could not resist and looked again. The impersonator saw me; he greeted me by addressing me, waving his hat, and bowing deeply. I had grown irreversibly old, since my reaction was to leave the balcony and go into the foyer. Asimakis and a few others followed me. A babel was heard outside, but I did not go back out. They told us in a little while that some people had pulled off the mask of the impersonator and had chased him uptown. He turned out to be a student named Lombardos. I commented in jest that he had the same name as the leader of a rival Zakynthian *komitato* of old, a brilliant politician to be sure. The incident ended there.

The local newspapers wrote about these happenings. Had you by any chance heard? I was embittered by the discovery that, in dedicating many of my works that were published from time to time to the younger generations, I had come close to forgetting the familiar goings-on. I am speaking of the symbolic death of the father by his son and heir. I had seen the drop of blood by studying the theater and had verified it by observing what went on around me; still, I was hurt when this happened to concern me.

A thought for the present: if you had seen me ridiculed thus (I mean according to the code of a custom which implies that the mask is not to be forcibly removed—otherwise, what would be the point of anonymity on these pages?), the excusable caricature might have dispelled or reduced your fears (if I finally admit that you were overtaken by fear and not by something else that I could not understand).

Listen to this also: I found myself in an orchard—with high stone walls, darkened by the hearts of ivy. In the orchard I cultivated a small tree. Orange tree, you had an aversion to violent winds as you shone your leaves at teeth and fingers. I wanted the golden apple of your love—even though we were lost.

To be able to make the trip of the farmer to the Ithaca of his lonely tree, I studied your former countenance. So you would not grow old, I used to silently recite the spells and exorcisms of the common people. To find your soul, I studied the souls of other people, at different periods in time.

Do not ever be ashamed that we fell in love.

Was I a man of my time? I think so. I owe this primarily to the fact that I studied older times.

Becoming has two mirrors facing each other: the uninterrupted past and the fleeting present. In how many ways is one mirrored in the words that have lived on in order to continue living to infinity?

I am arriving at the conclusion that the projection of love as something very old was for me even more necessary than the prospect of its future—quite possibly, even of its need to be defeated.

How old?

My heart condition had gotten worse. I remember the acrimonious description of some newspaper—that I cooled my already cold talk with frequent drinks of water and the breathing of a fan. Someone wrote—in the same newspaper or in another?—that I was an impostor and that I lived on other people's money. Defending me, some other papers wrote that I alone lived my political life without taking bribes, which means in a paradise: steadfast, unselfish, very theoretical.

At the last elections I was not elected deputy, even though I had more votes than all the previous times, because, according to the new electoral law, the electoral districts were expanded and the number of required votes was raised considerably.

So was this the reason?

Rose-colored marble trims. Dark wood on the benches and the podium. Tall doors with marble pediments and crimson drapes. Wall candleholders with open double wings. The polygonal clock over the presidential chair. Black suits, white shirts, and ties.

The government building of the Greeks: theater and hypocrites.

I lived there. I gave speeches. I pay off the honor.

The silence of a professional speaker is not the outcome of a moment but the spinning wheel on which his life winds. I began writing to you by pulling at the end of the red yarn. If you do not see it this way, certainly you are not to blame.

I ask for your indulgence.

It is dark and I must leave.

Your hand on the hollowness of a starlit night. Star, where will you lead me?

Yes, at the last elections, I was not elected deputy, and a few months later Asimakis died also. Asimakis died.

I lost the world.

To see you. Why, why in so many years had I not dared?

To see you, Louisa, to see you.

31 december 1888
on the ship, at night

I came pursued by the loss of my friend. I came pursued, as at other times I was pursued by the gendarmerie of the king. I came pursued by the ghost of a revolution which wanted to be reborn with different features. I came pursued by life that was drying up (and I could not remain composed when faced with either the slightest form of it or the greatest). I came pursued with a lump in my throat. I came, Louisa, to see you.

Normally, I should have waited in the city until dusk, walking up and down in the squares and in the arcades of the major streets and along the waterfront with the beautiful buildings and churches. I tried it, but it was impossible for me to measure, step by step, the cell of a summer evening. However, I counted the years I had not seen you to be twenty-seven.

I got in a buggy that was waiting on Strata Marina, provoking with its dark bulk the transparent patience of the hour. I ordered the coachman to hurry as fast as he could to your country place but to stop first at the home of the landowner. While he was hurrying, I was tormented by something like asphyxiation, and I tried to get some air by waving a handkerchief. I put it to better use by wiping my sweat. If only I had a little water. The coachman did not have any either. The horse that pulled us had the color of cinnamon. When I got down, I concentrated on remembering the color, looking at it until it disappeared.

I started walking on the dirt road, next to the stone fence. I walked on one of the two grooves made by the wheels of coaches and carts. All around, dry grass, olive trees, vineyards, and amaranths. I walked with unsteady steps. Phrases of an old piece of writing about a trip to the Aegean that I had taken in my youth pecked at my mind—as they are doing now while I am writing to you. I prayed that I find you mine and kind.

God finally smiled at last.

Islands of the Aegean, breathe freely, speaking to one another like your beautiful maidens with the white necks and the dark eyes, when they sit along the seashore at sunset, waiting for the seafaring lover to come from afar.

My love shivers sweetly, like the clean wave that cools your breasts.

But the wave, oh, maiden, answered you with Sappho's last sigh.

A hymn of angels, written on earth.

This great icon of God.

I saw you from afar. My hands grabbed the steel lances that protected the entrance of your garden and drowned in the jasmine that had grown bushy in the gaps of their hold. Hair that I once had adorned with jasmine flowers: I bent my head down like a slave. My legs were ready to run away; but they did not—not before seeing you again.

You yourself were distant. You were standing at the edge of the path leading to the house. The pebbles of the path shone brightly between the two rows of cypress trees. (To remind us, you had said, of the immortality of lovers. To remind us of the love of Eros and Thanatos, I had answered.) How many? I think five steps going up. You went up the steps and stood on the covered porch. You were talking with a woman who had been working for you for a long time. She had grown old, and I hardly remembered her.

The woman left. I saw you alone but protected by the arch

of the middle bow that leaned on the top step, supported by two slender columns. The whitewash stood its ground, with all the light that the summer day had poured on it, against the darkness that nonchalantly took over the garden. With the same nonchalance, you also touched the white wall. You stood your ground against a strange premonition, but nothing around you seemed different. Shortly, the light of the whitewash died out. You also disappeared behind the door. You came back with a lamp, a book, and a pair of eyeglasses. You put the lamp on the table and sat down on the cane armchair. You opened the book. You began to read, once more protected by the light of the lamp that draped you in a crystal cloak.

A dog barked far away. I pushed the gate and proceeded to the pebbled walk. You heard it creaking. You raised your eyes, taking off your glasses. Then you stood up. A man was coming from the path with the cypress trees. You set the book on the table. You brought your hand to your heart. Your eyes were wide open. I came near you. Your hand left your breast and darted in front of you, forbidding the man, alive or dead, from approaching.

You recognized me. Your knees caved in, and you sank in the armchair, as your hand hung motionless. I took it, and I held it tenderly.

We looked at each other's eyes twenty-seven whole years. Our hands held on tightly even beyond the last minute.

I sum up. I came to Zakynthos, I stayed in town for a short while, I hurried with a one-horse buggy to your country place, I walked babbling up to the gate, I approached, I took your hand. I embraced you and we kissed.

That kiss.

It plunged me at once into rooms with high ceilings and filled to the top with jasmine. Thus I was not able to see whether your beautiful furnishings were surrounding us or whether other people lived nearby and we should after all be embarrassed. I was looking toward the side from which a beam of white light was shining. But there was no window nor a way to desert you again. I was listening to the rain for hours—summer downpours were frequent, the type that force the ground to remember happy people. And we were the most happy, buried and warm under the white jasmine that was tossed about like down everywhere. Recalling the sacred flood, we were learning, even at this late hour, that there never was an ark other than the kiss.

So had we been saved?

I can even claim, Louisa, that, as long as we were together, all the words that render the world recognizable escaped me. I do not know anymore what color your dresses were. I do not know if jasmine flowers strung together on a thread crowned your hair, or if it was adorned by old cinnamon quills. I know, nevertheless, that no caress was granted autonomy from the lighted tyranny of our embrace on the porch, which did not allow any type of liberation; that an archetypal trust was leading us to avoid whatever in love has to do with insignificant things—those to which we had assigned the most possessive names when we were young; that an angel, panting, wise, sheltering, smiled down at us. We assumed it was the forgiveness of paradise for the punishment it had imposed on the knowledge of a young couple many years ago. I still remember that I was holding you like a new mother nurses her baby, loving it even before she had given it birth. Not only did I not know the age of the body I had in my arms, but neither did it lead me to the Upper or the Lower World. I asked myself then what perchance I knew of either one of them, I, the insignificant one.

Not even their words.

I cannot estimate how long we lived embracing. However, one

evening comes back to mind glimmering: when we were sailing in the galaxy on a flat-bottomed boat, like those the fishermen used in the Maremma. Lowering our hands, we caught stars. Or perhaps jasmine?

Then I thought that the way humans measure time never had anything to do with the temporality of their love. The time of love was always universal while the measuring of earthly time had been trapped in cycles.

The memory of our embrace on the porch came to assist me in my meditation. Quiet sobs began to strike their own pendulum while the twenty-seven lost years measured the entirety of their duration in one glance of ours: benevolent echoes, sweet, as if from the mechanical theater of time. I am speaking of an old tall clock of dark wood chiseled in bands that I had seen once in the cathedral of a medieval city. As soon as a small unit of earthly time passed, bright-colored wooden figures came out to parade around the clock and disappeared within it again. At every cycle, the sobs of time were heard—benevolent, sweet, like ours.

The time of love is universal; but it gives way and becomes perceptible just when it discovers its own measure, which is different for each love. The density of twenty-seven lost years in one glance: henceforth, let that measure our share in the infinity of lovers.

One day we happened to be on a ship that was taking us to Patras. I could not see the blue of either the sky or the sea. A diffused pale light crystallized into small clouds and crests of waves. The northwest wind, the mistral, piled the jasmine in the hallways, the sitting room, the cabins, filling the pillows of the beds with its pure down.

We approached, but I was not able to see even the familiar landscape of the city. The morning sun concealed it behind its slanted rays. Myriads of jasmine flowers climbed on them; I was reminded of a bridal veil. The city concealed its face from the bridegroom who was coming. I wondered what was the meaning of this last disguise.

Cities live longer than their people. They live even longer than the vision that once gave them birth and the hand that built them impressive. Their strength is the indifference of matter for all those who dwell in them. Their weapon, a time of greater range. These things I knew, more or less. Suddenly, however, I saw behind the voile the deeper fear of the cities: it is the fear of revolutions, the same fear as the fear of love. Like a bride that exorcises evil, Patras had draped itself in veils to welcome us.

I could not feel anymore whether it was jasmine or ashes that touched me. I am speaking of the ashes that came from the flames of the rebelling city as far out as the ship of refugees, the ship on which I was born, exactly on these waters. I tried to find your face, as I then tried to find my mother's breast. Would the future ever come, as I had preached it?

I doubted it more and more, for as we crossed the city, everything was concealed behind a white paper war: theater, hotels, houses, banks, shops, and streets. There was no human being, not even a remembrance of a human being. Whom should I ask about the future? Thus I took you with me to whirl about in empty white streets. We arrived at your house dancing the waltz of our first meeting. The door to the outside had been jammed by piles of flowers. Finally we opened it. As we expected, your home was overflowing with jasmine also. Embracing, we went to clear the piano. You played the sonata that served as a guardian over you after our last separation. The petals absorbed the sound, and its sadness was not heard.

At that moment I asked myself where the two of us belonged, having been denied many things and having allowed even more. You smiled at me. Again in a short while I asked myself if the temptation and the experience of our love spun together the yarn of pleasure and the yarn of our destruction; and if, for this reason, the yarn of the labyrinth is always two ply. Then, Louisa, you closed the piano and looked at me, as if to tell me that only the foolish in our situation ask such questions—as if you were telling me to get away from the riddle of this city.

We were again in Zakynthos. I am not insisting that we had left it. It would have been dangerous for us to leave the isolation of an island. More dangerous yet to go away from the shade of the commanding poet; standing on Strani Hill, he was seeing the smoke cloud of the battle on the opposite shore. He was weeping, arming us forever with the goodness of his verses.

True, we were not at all preoccupied with smoke clouds and battles. It is just that his sigh, like a child's soul, shone among the jasmine: to show me that you were always the betrothed who teaches the young by prophesying the charm of her old age, and that, simultaneously, you had not stopped using an imperishable youth in the yarn of your wrinkles; to show me also something more significant. I shall not shy away from mentioning it: the only thing that cast lightly its shadow, the only thing that at moments I desired even more than desiring you was to have a child together—a small child, as in fairy tales.

Because lovers are not beings of everyday life either but creations of old fairy tales.

Ten of twelve. I have just enough time to arrange all that I wrote to you these last few days in my portfolio. On it I shall write your real name with a plea that it be given to you. So, only a couple of words.

Dedicated for years to the discipline of speech, I realize that I was blinded by the splendor of some irrational hours. I was thus benefited by the vision of the blind and bewildered in a world that suddenly changed from familiar to unfamiliar.

The time consents to my ignorance once more—whether you

were only a face, or in one face I summed up all the others; whether you came as a vision or I embraced you as a woman; whether you are now dead or still unborn.

I was in love with the siren of a certain revolution. She will now blow out her first one hundred candles in the sea, and she is waiting for me at the celebration so we can embrace each other in love.

So long, Louisa, whoever you may be.

EXODOS

july 1897
patras

Since early this morning an old world raised me on its wings. It had me counting and recounting the years. Each time I find them to be exactly eight and a half. "Exactly" stops on New Year's, when he jumped into the sea.

His messenger came to my house this morning. He was wearing a dark suit, white collar, tie, and top hat: ordinary clothes and rather old. His hair was adorned with fine lines in the only color used by time. He brought me the first part of *Politikós Agón* fresh from the publisher. He himself had written the introduction. His name was Vasilis Kalliontzis. He stayed for quite a while. From him I learned that Mr. Drakoulis at Oxford and the newspaper *Neológos Patrón* hailed the publication of *Politikós Agón* in favorable terms. He promised that he would come again soon. I hope to see him again.

As soon as he left, I took the pamphlet in my hands. It was small, and I thought that I would read it quickly. But I was overcome with tears, and it took me a long time to read it. I do not know how many hours. From the outset the old world took me on an unbearable journey—something that I shall not call either truth or love or youth. Perhaps a flame—a flame that shone once in a while in loving eyes, sweet like a spring orchard. I wanted him. I thought that, as we grow old, we do not want anyone, or that one is not torn to pieces by wanting. But it was a mistake.

I finally read all of the introduction. I did not find even one line of writing about our long-lasting affair. I wonder if it is because of a mistake or because this is the way it should be. I am thinking that he must have made this request. I come to that conclusion when I consider that he left forever without leaving a word for me, the only word, "farewell." I do not reproach him; he must have had his reasons. But I find today's silence exaggerated and unjust. After a certain point everyone knew about our love affair. A light in his eyes, a tone of voice, a reverie gave him away. Such signs do not escape people's attention, nor, most certainly, the attention of his friend and biographer. Kalliontzis's decision to come early this morning to give me the first pamphlet indicates that he was not ignorant with regard to this matter. That he did not write about it or that he did not hint at it in the slightest way during his visit does not matter. But I did not open up such a conversation either. I would not have even if I had already read the introduction. Most certainly he must have made this request. The official silence. Why am I looking for my name in his biography, a name that has remained invisible for a whole lifetime?

The way he left me so many times was unjust and excessive. I am not saying that he had an obligation to me; he found me married to another. What am I looking for, and for what reason? I suffered, however, every time a wind took him away, sometimes to Athens, other times to foreign lands, the last time to his wretched end. Better that I do not count them. He used to run away as soon as love would take hold of us, as if pursued by the fear of tenderness—along with all his real persecutors. I could see him; he was tormented. I thought that sometimes he placed me also next to the fairy-tale creatures of his mind. While I loved him, I can say that I was afraid of him then, as if he were studying something indeterminably bad. But a kiss pulled us quickly to the other extreme of our life.

Besides, what was real in this love? That I saw him after a

moment that had lasted twenty-seven full years perhaps? Or that we abandoned ourselves to the conversation of an ineffable love? What can I believe of the twilight that interprets the dawn? Is a sprig of jasmine enough? Oh, wings, lift me high. . . . Away from the absence of his "farewell." I know the difficulty of one word in love—nor do I want his word for egotistical reasons. He had told me and written to me so many. It is just that sometimes the absence of only one word weighs as much as all the rest. Besides, "farewell" is a kiss, not just any word.

He was always a loner and secretive. I always had to guess. There were moments when I preferred that he be far away and that I think of him rather than have him near me. He and the man that I married were opposites in this respect. I had loved him too, but, I dare say, in a very different way. Until today, nothing has been clarified with regard to the assassination, not even whether he was attacked by bandits or by others—as if the truth should not be made known since so many years have gone by. Let me stop thinking of dates; they do not bring relief. It is strange that they both had violent deaths, as if their ceased friendship always had the need of a common reference. Why am I thinking of this now? In my mind I have them reconciled. May their forms, reconciled on their own in heavenly walks, think well of me.

Yes, the messenger brought me good news. I touch the pamphlet, and I shiver as if I were touching the beloved hand. I picture him handsome. In his own way, however. There was something in his look that raised him to the lightning of forbidden knowledge in order to cast him from there in the darkness of the most banal despair. This something pulled him to a sea of torments, distancing him from the boat of a conventional life. He also had the need of a mother, of a wife, of a way, but he called all these things vain. I was not able to untie the knot; other sirens had put their spell on him. I agree—they were beautiful ideas, but they required so much dedication. He had to believe that he was (and he was actually) the destined, the one chosen by fate. Otherwise, he would not have been able to endure—just as he could not endure the shared space and the defeat of love: love's victims, leaning on one another's shoulders and walking who knows where, until they find the measure of time exact once again and their words even more exact in the absolute emptiness. Of course, now his works are published, and people are writing about his life, with the financial support of the city and its citizens, however. Present conditions do not help. There is war again with the Turks, the disbanding of the army, bankruptcy. I foresee that the publication will have to be stopped in the middle for many and various reasons. Where will immortality be then, that "be it so" which would give rest to his soul? Not even the most commonplace immortality, the immortality of having a son.

For me, it would have been enough if, instead of his son, I had held his own dead body. The newspapers at the time wrote that the sea had washed it out on Porto Heli, where it was quickly buried. In the beginning I did not dare. Later on—I am not going to count the years again—I went there. No one knew where the grave of this sinner was, or they did not trust the woman who had an unconsecrated union with him. They knew everything about us. They did not comment, but they did not open up in conversation either. I returned without accomplishing anything, and I had to be bedridden a second time, for, earlier, that terrible January when the news first appeared, I had become ill also. When I was able to stand up on my own again, I went through all the rituals of a widow in grief. I knew them well. In Patras people looked at me sideways because I was grieving for my lover, and some avoided me. I must say that no one insulted me; I would not have forgotten it if they had. Yes, and recently Londos proposed to the city council that a monument be erected. His proposal was accepted, but nothing has been done yet. I shall say this again: knowing that I would be able to bend over the body with which I used to come together in love and breathe jasmine would be painful for me. I am tormented as if suddenly I were tied to a vendetta, which, although I have to, I am not able to carry out. I just repeat the lines that Gabrielidis wrote for him that terrible January in his Athenian newspaper. I repeat them like an oath: that he was one of the noblest figures of modern Greece; that he was buried in the Romaic chaos, where intelligence, originality, genius, and a bright mind sink; that our youth should latch on to the works of the man who was a type of Quinet and Michelet for Greece.

There are times when I think that maybe he did not love me enough. I understand that the words of love sometimes exceed the feelings themselves, without intending any harm, as if this verbal exaggeration were necessary. He must have reckoned that, although I liked his ideas, they never attracted me to a similar type of bondage; that is what I shall call it—but whoever heard of a woman involved in such matters in this place and especially a few decades back? The fact is that, when I was widowed, he did not dare to take me with him—by marrying me or otherwise. Was he afraid perhaps because I was getting old? Or did he not love me anymore? That is why I lived so many years in Zakynthos alone. It was not for me to make this request. Between us there was no definite end, but the pieces never got glued together sturdily again. I do not know if the women with whom he kept company in Athens and in Europe were like me, or whether they mingled in the theater and in politics. I did not ask him, nor did I ever write to him of the countless comments well-meaning people let drop near me, as if meaning no harm. He did likewise. If there were something of great significance, he would have told me, or I would have sensed it. That is why I felt badly when I saw that Kalliontzis refers to the Englishwoman in his introduction but is silent about our love. I never understood the rumored engagement. It did not agree with anything that I had loved about him. However, since he did not tell me anything about it, I do not know what exactly took place. The reference to her in the introduction without mention of her name seems to be an intentional mistake on the part of his biographer, of his only biographer for the time being—certainly not because I prefer things this way. If in the future he is fortunate to have other biographers also, I hope that they will be more careful with the so-called truth—either everything or nothing; otherwise, what does the word mean? I have only this to add: even if he had told his friend to keep silent about the one and to bring up the other, I shall forgive him. He was so sensitive, so dreamy and eccentric that I do not wonder why admirable women fell in love with him. Why did he choose to suffer with me between grief and pleasure?

After so many years, I would have been able to trace a cool response in his letters. Do I claim to be calm and cool? I shudder at the memory of these letters, but more so at the fact that none of them survived the sin of its existence. I know, I made him bleed thousands of times, tearing up every one of his letters in a thousand pieces. That is what I was aiming to do. Lack of courage on the part of a woman with courageous feelings? Words, words. Just as he left without leaving a word for me, in the same way, when I heard that he was gone, that he was lost forever, I destroyed all his words, whatever I had or did not have. Among his letters were some sent to him by known individuals and several old newspapers that he had entrusted me with a long time ago. For years he did not ask for anything. I assumed that they were useless, and I destroyed them too. For years—the years we stayed away from each other, as if absence or pursuit was the reason our love gushed forth, in order to dry up in the presence of my homeless knight.

I went on living. I tried to forget everything, words and letters. I remembered only his beautiful handwriting, but I was not able to find the pulse of his handwritten page again, nor the warmth of his voice. I believed that I had forgotten all that I had to forget in order to live—until today, when, suddenly, archangelic wings grabbed me early in the morning and lifted me up high to once again see him arriving from foreign lands to the beat of today: the garden stopping, the hour trembling, and he approaching from the rows of cypress trees. Oh, let him look at me in the eyes countless of years. Let him embrace me so I can sink in jasmine. Let him kiss me, so we can finally bring our life to an end.

He sat in the chair across from me. July was sending forth hot green vapors. Even though it was summer, the day before it had been raining ceaselessly. He did not take off his cape. Small drops shone on his forehead. I could not tell if it was perspiration or rain—if not seawater. He reached out and took the pamphlet from the table next to him. He was happy as he gleaned sentences from his friend's introduction and from his own youthful writing that followed: "*A hymn of angels, written on earth. This great icon of God.*" He raised his eyes and looked at me. How can I say it? He smiled in the same wonderful way.

Shortly he turned back to the front cover of the pamphlet. The mask of tragedy touched the mask of comedy in between dense, beautifully drawn ringlets. He began to count the pages. He read the names of his friends once again and his acknowledgments. I heard him whisper the date of the last words that were written by his own hand: 28 December 1888. He threw a quick glance at the dedication of his work to the first of the new generations which time would show that it distinguished itself, and he fixed his glance on the same page, exactly under the dedication, on two verses by Dante, placed within a linear frame. With his face lit up, he read to me:

Ricordati di me . . . .
. . . . maremma mi disfece.

He became silent. His eyes, illuminated by his beloved poetry and the secret flame that consumed him, remembered mine once again. He asked me if I had understood. Understood what, I wondered. If I had understood, he repeated, the way he interpreted the two half verses—because he had made a mistake in writing them down in order to play a well-intentioned trick on his biographers. And he burst into hearty laughter.

His voice. I thought that perhaps I was not hearing it, that perhaps I only imagined it, that perhaps the spell of the moon had led me straight back to its erotic tone. He asked me for a third time, and then I realized what he was telling me. I whispered that I did not have a chance to familiarize myself with the pamphlet since Kalliontzis had brought it only this morning. He remained silent for a moment. Did his mind wander off to his good friend? He asked me again insistently if I at least remembered from what part of *The Divine Comedy* the above verses were taken. Annoyed, I answered, no, I did not remember. His countenance darkened, as if I had lowered the wick of the lamp that lit the room. It quickly lit up again as soon as he started speaking.

The secret that he wanted to conceal in these six words by Dante had to be revealed sometime. Let someone know it. He was happy that I would be the one. I shivered then, I, as if the woman he had loved had anything to do with me, as if all these things were nothing more than a way of saying farewell, of sharing an embrace. I could not speak of our kiss as a kiss anymore. I listened to him attentively all the hours he stayed with me; but during those same hours, I imagined him just as I had known him—as if our love was in need of a postscript.

First of all, he did not consider himself suicidal. He wished that I would see for myself with my own eyes that he did not belong to that category—at least not to the category of people described in the Seventh Circle of the Inferno: metamorphosed to a dense forest of souls with the branches of the trees twisted and knotty, trees bearing no fruit but full of pitch-black leaves and prickly thorns. He, however, had come to find me with the same appearance that he had in times past. I could see for myself, and I should not forget. (And I, the woman who is I, said to myself, with the same appearance that I had at other times filled with kisses.)

He belonged, he said, among those who had a violent death. Their souls are recounted in *Purgatorio,* the very conical mountain on the only island of the southern hemisphere of the earth, as they are burning and coveting the rose of *Paradiso.* Out of this crowd, of those who have had a violent death, the soul of a noble contessa, Pia de Tholomé, came to speak to the living visitor of Hades.

He interrupted his narration to tell me that specifically from the few and bitter words of the contessa Pia de Tholomé he had dared to borrow the two half verses. More important, he had dared to copy one word incorrectly. But before he explained his action to me, he asked me if he had ever spoken or written to me about this unlucky woman; he remembered something, without being sure what it was exactly.

I motioned to him that he had not. He turned silent and appeared disturbed, as if he could not believe that in all those years he had not spoken to the woman who had touched his life about a woman who had also touched him, even though she had been dead for many centuries. He put the pamphlet that he had been holding affectionately on the table next to him and concentrated as he tried to remember the old story from beginning to end.

They killed Pia de Tholomé, he began shortly, in the region of Italy called the Maremma. It was not very far from Pisa, where, if I remembered, he had studied. Vast marshes had given the region this particular name. He happened to visit the place with a group of fellow students at the time when they had started to drain the marshes. The place, always cursed to bring forth snakes and fatal fevers, had become haunted since the death of the contessa. Dante forced us, the forgetful ones, to remember her soul always as the most lonely soul in all of the Lower World because she spoke and said to him

> . . . *Remember me, I am Pia;*
> *Siena gave me birth, Maremma was my ruin.*

He became silent for a moment, long enough to consider the verses again, and continued, saying that their motif could be a digression from Virgil's well-known verses: "Mantua gave me birth, Calabria carried me off." Besides, Virgil's ghost had accompanied Dante on his trip through Hades. The alteration of these words as they left the lips of the contessa was accompanied by a description of her own troubles using the allusions and abstractions that are normally necessary when a dead person speaks with a living one—exactly as is the case with good poetry, he added, and his eyes sparkled.

Pia de Tholomé did not report her assassin to Dante. She avoided naming him, although she knew very well who he was. Furthermore, she carefully avoided naming anything or anyone other than herself and the two places that have a just and equal share of a human name: the place of birth and the place of death. As for her assassin, she said only that he was the one who had given her a very expensive ring before the marriage ceremony. That is why she did not have anyone in the Upper World who loved and remembered her anymore. So she begged Dante to remember her when he returned to the light of the sun and had rested after his long journey.

The wrinkle between his eyebrows deepened—another sign that he was trying to remember. If the fancies of an immaterial memory did not deceive him, he added, the commentators on the above verses named the contessa's assassin, although she had avoided doing so. What is the motive of the biographers and the commentators? he turned and asked me roughly. Is it only a matter of justice that has not been attended to? Without waiting for an answer, he continued softly, saying that her assassin was her husband, Nello, or Paganello, a well-to-do official, owner of other castles as well as the castle of Pietra in the Tuscan Maremma. Either because Pia had committed a wrongdoing or because he suspected her of infidelity, or because—and most likely—he wanted to marry a beautiful widow of noble birth, Nello led Pia to the castle of the Maremma and gave an order to do away with her.

His order was carried out so well, according to what people said, that no one knew how she was killed. Some maintained that, while the contessa was standing at the window, someone sent by Nello grabbed her by the legs and threw her in the deep swamp below. Nothing was heard about her from that point on; but the spot on the hill where the castle of the Maremma stood was named the Leap of the Contessa.

When he had gone with his fellow students to the Maremma, the boatman showed them the spot with the above name. The young men wanted to know more, and, as he was rowing, he related to them the story of Pia de Tholomé, which had taken place seven centuries earlier. His version of the story did not differ from the most up-to-date commentaries, while at the same time showing great compassion for the contessa's loneliness in both the Upper and the Lower Worlds.

Old stories that come out of dates, faces, and places, just as the snake comes out of its skin. That is why they should not disturb me, he said, observing that I was wiping my sweating palms with a handkerchief. Perhaps the thought of the snake changing shirts increased my perturbation? It should not. He added gently that I should relax, his glance caressing my face to the point that I could not bear it anymore, and I said, "I love you." But my words dissolved before they left my teeth; they had not managed to change their shirt. At least he gave no indication that he heard them.

He could finally talk to me about his intentional mistake. It was very simple, so most would consider it a typographical error or a slip of memory. He had changed the word "Maremma" by not capitalizing the first letter. The word appeared in Italian in this form also—*maremma*—and it meant, as I was probably aware (and he stopped to ask me if people still wrote and spoke Italian well in our region), a coastal place, usually at the mouth of a river, full of marshes and sandy dunes. The region near Patras, for example, would give me the best picture of such a place—the swamps that used to be there in between stretches of cultivated land before they were drained.

He ventured to meddle with the word for many reasons. He did not want himself inseparably associated with that specific Italian location. He did not wish to be weighed down by one more, although insignificant, guilt. Second, the word suggested the city of Patras without naming it. The most profound reason, however (for which he had chosen the two verses, leaving out quite a few words and, with his mistake, generalizing the meaning of a place name), was that he absolutely did not want any proper name to exist, not his own, not the name of a place, not the name of someone else. By leaving out of the Dantean verses every specific reference and, furthermore, by concealing his own name, he aspired to approach the ultimate, the ideal form of symbolism, that which exists only in anonymity, so that there would be no name, and no interpretation—the perfect flow of a life that did not play itself out in the stereotypical anonymity of a retired life but in the necessity of an exemplary life. Therefore, in the necessity of an exemplary death as well. No one would be able to accuse someone else as his assassin if he were not a face but the meaning of a word. And again, he said, looking at me, his words should not disturb me; everything was in the sphere of a different type of understanding. May it also be a different type of justice.

I got up awkwardly to bring the bottle with the liqueur and

two small glasses. He appeared to be lost in thought. Returning with the tray, I could hear the crystal translating the tremor of my hands to low, short, incessant sounds. Could he also hear the tremolo? I left the tray on the table. However, I yearned to touch him so much that I continued to shiver.

He had talked to me as a person in the midst of crying begins to talk to oneself. I realized that he had come as he used to come, chased by the scarcity of tenderness, which he could not stand. If he left now (and how could he stay, since he was confined to his destiny?), he would be lost forever. He did not have another secret to reveal to me, and, consequently, no more tears. I felt sorry for him, but I was not overcome by compassion. I just wished to touch him. However, I realized that it was not possible to verify his presence even with my little finger—since he was so aloof, so resigned to his wishes.

I poured some liqueur into a glass and offered it to him with an uncertain movement of my hand—beseeching the touch of his hand. I wonder if he noticed. He neither spoke nor reached to take the glass. As I was tired of holding out my arm, I left the glass beside him. I picked up my own glass decisively and drank the liqueur in one gulp. A myriad jasmine flowers bloomed inside of me. I wonder if he smelled them also. I asked him to forgive me for interrupting him, offering him a drink in a most unmannerly way, without first putting it on the tray. I must have made him uncomfortable; but I did not ask him to forgive me for longing to touch him.

He smiled. He murmured something like "bittersweet harmless reptile." My mind wandered again to the empty shirt of a reptile, and I shuddered, while he explained that there still were one or two minor differences in the half verses of a grammatical nature and explainable in terms of the flow of the language over several centuries, which differences did not mean anything special. As for the words "Remember me," if I wanted to, I could regard them as being addressed to the woman he had loved. If I wanted, he repeated, I could consider his use of the singular as the touch of fingers, as a "farewell." However, it was small-minded for one to consider that in a sentence so empty of names, of places, and of people—in the shirt of such a sentence, he insisted, looking straight into my eyes—there is one and only one addressee. The singular here implies the plural: the "I" implies "we"; "thou" implies "you"; "he" implies "they." If for no other reason than that a few friends remember him after a hundred years or so and talk about him in a mountainous Achaian village while eating and drinking wine on a cool summer evening, with the grapes hanging in perfect clusters from the arbor; if for no other reason than that other gatherings of friends remember him in a distant and uncertain future in enclosed gardens behind pale or dark red neoclassical homes in Patras, the last homes that will still be standing, their memory lost—gardens and tall arches whose former charms he knew well; or, at least, so the loners of libraries, of ideas, of love will remember him once in a while: his friends.

He got carried away once again by his wish for his future, he confessed. He wished I would remain good to him. (Is there anyone from beyond who is not overtaken by such a wish?) This wish gave him the right to entrust me with the question that had rather stubbornly overtaken him of late: in wishing to have a future, in other words, in wishing to be recalled by the living once in a while, was he not approaching poetry by a different road perhaps? We should not forget the clarity of the archetype: Pia de Tholomé secured her future by way of art, the only resurrection.

But it would be a good idea not to nourish too many hopes, he continued. He could not believe anymore in the miracle of art either in the Upper or in the Lower World. Besides, who would be worthy of remembrance? Only allusions and extracts, rarely an awareness of a work and a life fastened together with the bonds of love and death. He did not deny that many times he had a chance to verify fragments of his older but also of his more recent written work by observing souls in the darkness, or, while still living, in the light. He lived with these fragments, knowing that he could not measure up to even their shortest syllable. This would take place even more rarely in the future, however—if in a short time no one would remember his work, his life. (By "no one," he also implied the few friends and the gatherings of friends in the garden, as well as his loner friends.) At last let him confess, he sighed, that his ambition, the ambition of a revolutionary, never was to be consumed by so few.

Again, it is possible that lethe was precisely the result of the way he had lived, had written, had loved, and had died, he continued more calmly—a way that, if most people do not shy away from being instructed by it, will stubbornly attempt to forget it. He, therefore, should not complain.

His wish for his future is something else; definitely something else.

He took out the watch that I had given him. He opened the cover with the engraved rosette and looked at the time. I saw the fine black hands united on the Latin twelve. To be exact, the minute hand had moved on slightly. The watch must have stopped because, while he held it open for a little while, the minute hand did not move. However, I realized that it was close to dawn by the low sounds of the city as it was waking up and stirring in its bed. He told me that it was already midnight and that he had to go. Its first hundred years, he continued, without explaining to me what he meant, proved to be fruitless. So, after the embrace of the hands of the watch, after the hours pass and I see the rose-colored dawn behind the mountain tops of Panachaiko, then, if I had loved him, I should remember him again: anonymous, perhaps because of a useless choice, but lavishly well known in his time. For all we know, he said, closing the silver cover and observing the gleaming metal of a ray incising the crimson velvet drapes, perhaps all these things took place because he was born, and thus had to die, on the water. Not in Pisa, nor in Patras, nor in Athens. In the perfect anonymity of the waves. Their blue is more murky than a symbolic life, more fluid than an acquired name, deeper than the body that brings you forth and the earth that wants you back. He was not the only one, nor was he alone. I could bring to mind his companions: how many revolutionaries, how many beloved, how many poets in the blue polis of a *maremma*. . . .

The light was bothering him. I rose to close the drapes. When I returned, he was no longer sitting in the armchair.

Author's Notes

The title of the novel *Tha hypográpho Loui* [*I Shall Sign as Loui*] comes from the first letter of Andreas Rigopoulos to Edgar Quinet (Patras, 6–18 August 1856), specifically from the following sentence: "Au lieu de mon nom je signerai Loui" ("Instead of my name, I shall sign as Loui"). This letter was published by Roger Milliex in his "Eksi anékdotes epistolés tou A. Rigópoulou pros ton Edgar Quinet" ["Six Unpublished Letters of A. Rigopoulos to Edgar Quinet"], *Praktiká tis Akademías Athenón* [*Proceedings of the Academy of Athens*] 63 (1988): 140–63.

The translation of Dante's verses (*Purgatorio*, v.133–34)

... Θυμήσου εμένα πού είμαι η Πία
η Σιένα μ' έκανε, μὲ ξέκανε η Μαρέμα. ...

[... *Remember me, I am Pia:*
Siena gave me birth; Maremma was my ruin. ...]

belongs to George Seferis, who places them next to the original

... *ricorditi di me che son la Pia:*
Siena mi fé; disfecemi Maremma. ...

for the purpose of commenting on verses 293 and 294 of *Erimi Hóra* [*The Waste Land*] by T. S. Eliot (Athens: Ikaros, 2d ed., 1986, pp. 96, 144–45, 164) as Seferis himself translated them:

"Τὸ Χάιμπουρυ μ' ἔθρεψε. Τὸ Ρίτσμοντ καὶ τὸ Κιοὺ / μὲ ξέκαναν" ["Highbury bore me. Richmond and Kew / Undid me"].

The first part of the first Dantean verse and the second part of the second are used as an epigraph in *Politikós Agón: Philologiká kai Politiká érga tou Andréou Rigopoúlou, ek Patrón* [*Political Struggle: Literary and Political Works of Andreas Rigopoulos of Patras*], published by his friend Vasilios G. Kalliontzis (Patras: P. Eumorphopoulos's printing shop, the Phoenix, 1897). The epigraph is as follows:

Ricordati di me . . . .
. . . . maremma mi disfece.
—Dante

The parts of the book that are in quotation marks [or indented] and printed in italics are excerpts from the works of Andreas Rigopoulos.

The character of Louisa is entirely fictional.

Translator's Notes

7   *the Ionian Islands*   The islands along the western coast of Greece, which were for centuries part of the Venetian Empire and, subsequently, were governed by the French and, between 1815 and 1864, by the British. Many poets came from these islands, most of them educated in Italy and writing in demotic Greek, the spoken form of modern Greek (in contrast to *katharevousa*).

7   *katharevousa*   Throughout most of the nineteenth and twentieth centuries, *katharevousa* was designated as the "official" language, at least in its written form. *Katharevousa* implies "pure," that is, "cleansed" of foreign "impurities," and resembles ancient Greek in form.

10 *the onset of the war*   The Greek War of Independence against the Ottoman Empire. It began in 1821.

10 *Galaxidi*   A maritime town on the northern coast of the Corinthian Gulf.

11 *Philikoi*   Those belonging to the secret society Philiki Etairia (or simply Philiki), which was founded in Odessa in 1814 and whose purpose was the promotion of a revolution for the sake of liberating Greece from Ottoman rule.

11 *the famous Androutsos*   Odysseas Androutsos, one of the leading figures of the Greek War of Independence.

12 *Makriyannis*   Yannis Makriyannis (1797–1864) eventually became an army commander during the War of Independence. He is known primarily for his memoirs.

12 *the patron saint of Patras*   Saint Andreas.

12 *the mythical king of Ithaca*   Odysseus.

12 *a well-known ancient politician and admiral*   Themistocles.

12 *from Naupaktos to Preveza*   Naupaktos is a town on the northern coast of the Corinthian Gulf. It was formerly known in the West as Lepanto. Preveza is a seaside town on the Ionian Sea in western Greece.

14 *Kapodistrias*   Ioannis Kapodistrias (also known as Giovanni Antonio Capo D'Istria, 1776–1831), the first governor of modern Greece. He took office in 1828.

18 *the klephts*   Brigands of the countryside who played a decisive role during the War of Independence by joining ranks with the revolutionaries.

18 *kurus*   Turkish monetary units. One hundred kurus equals one Turkish pound or lira.

18 *the Orlofika*   Named after Count Orlov (1734–83), a Russian statesman and proponent of the Slavophile stance, which advocated the emancipation of the Christians from Ottoman rule. A revolt incited in the Peloponnesus in 1770 was initially successful, but it was put down by the Ottomans primarily because Russian help was slow in coming.

18 *the Moreas*   The Peloponnesus.

18 *ephor*   A tax collector.

19 *Kolokotronis*   Theodoros Kolokotronis (1770–1843), the most famous commander of the War of Independence.

19 *the Etairia*   Philiki Etairia.

24 *Othon's dethronement*   Othon (the Bavarian prince Otto) served as the first king of modern Greece, from 1833 to 1862.

30 *foustaneles*   Pleated kilts (singular *foustanela*), which were part of the traditional men's dress in southern Greece.

31 *the Danaans*   The Greeks.

31 *blameless, peaceful, and sinless*   This echoes the Greek Orthodox liturgical service. At one point, the priest prays that "the end of our life" be painless, blameless, and peaceful.

33 *Erimitis tou Halkomata*   The hermit of Halkomata.

34 *Ermoupolis*   The capital of the island of Syros.

36 *the governor's*   Refers to Ioannis Kapodistrias.

36 *the archaic language*   Katharevousa.

44 *yiantes*   A game of chance that children play with a wishbone. Two children pull at the opposite ends until the bone breaks. It invariably breaks unevenly. The child who ends up with the larger part is the winner. The loser has to keep silent and make requests in sign language (usually through the rest of the meal). If the winner catches the loser using actual words, he or she calls out *yiantes* and remains the winner. If the loser manages not to say anything for the specified amount of time, then he or she wins the game.

48 *the Risorgimento*   The movement for national unification.

50 *the Heptanesa*   The Ionian Islands are sometimes referred to as the Heptanesa since they (that is, the largest of them) are seven (*hepta*) in number.

51 *Kartería*   Fortitude.

58 *the Parisian Saint-Simonites*   Members of a society named after Claude Saint-Simon (1760–1825), French socialist thinker and writer.

59 *Garibaldi* Giuseppe Garibaldi (1807–82), an Italian revolutionary and strategist. During one of the many uprisings for Italian independence from foreign occupiers, he was sentenced to death and fled to South America. He returned fourteen years later, in 1848, and was very successful in leading small groups of soldiers to victory. Largely due to his successes, the kingdom of Italy (which, however, did not include Venice and Rome) was established in 1861 with Victor Emmanuel II as king. Garibaldi continued his revolutionary activity for the unification of Italy. Venice was acquired in 1866 and Rome in 1870.

63 *Chrónia Pollá* A greeting appropriate on many occasions but especially during the winter holidays and on birthdays and name days. Literally, it means "[Live] many years."

65 *kourambiethes* Butter cookies covered with powdered sugar, especially popular at Christmastime.

65 *kalikantzaroi* Mischievous goblins who, according to tradition, make their appearance on Christmas Eve, create havoc for the twelve days of Christmas, and are chased back underground on 6 January.

70 *Nauplion* Nauplion, on the east coast of the Peloponnesus, was the administrative seat of the Greek government until 1833, when Athens became the capital.

71 *Mesolongi* A town in southern mainland Greece, located on the northwestern shore of the Corinthian Gulf, not far from Patras.

78 *The Kanaris government* Konstantinos Kanaris (1790–1877), a follower of Kapodistrias, was prime minister from 1864 to 1865.

79 *Mazzini* Giuseppe Mazzini (1805–72), a literary critic and political leader. He fought for the liberation of Italy from foreign and domestic domination and for its unification under a republican government.

93 *I Ellinikí Siméa—Le Drapeau Hellénique* The Greek Flag.

95 *Les esclaves* The Slaves.

95 *the Megáli Idéa* A vision of Greece that included the irredentist territories that were not part of the Greek state, such as Thessaly, Epeirus, Anatolia, and Constantinople.

96 *the recent occupation of Piraeus* That is, by the French fleet during the Crimean War.

106 *To Méllon tis Patrídos* The Future of Our Country.

111 *the revolt of Thessaly and Epeirus* The districts of Thessaly and Epeirus were not liberated from Ottoman occupation during the Revolutionary War. Thessaly was eventually ceded to the Greek state in 1881. Southern Epeirus was united with Greece in 1914.

113 *Vlach shepherds* That is, of the Vlach race. The name is used to refer to descendants of the people of ancient Dacia or present-day Romania (Wallachia) who spread out in parts of neighboring countries, including Thessaly.

120 *the day of the Annunciation* The reference is to 25 March, which is also the anniversary of the Greek Revolution.

121 *the Bavarian king* King Othon.

122 *Karaiskakis's Camp* The reference is to a painting by Theodoros Bryzakis. Georgios Karaiskakis (1782–1827) was a leader in the Revolutionary War and a supporter of Kapodistrias.

124 *Victor Emmanuel*   Victor Emmanuel II (1820–78), a king of Sardinia and the first king of Italy.

140 *George's arrival*   George I, the king of the Hellenes (1845–1913), formerly a Danish prince. He came to the throne in 1863, after the dethronement of Othon.

142 *foresaw on the shoulder blades of sheep*   The reference is to the ancient Greek custom (now rarely seen) of studying the bones of cooked domestic animals for the purpose of foretelling the future.

157 *Emmanuel Roidis*   Emmanuel Roidis (1836–1904) was a Greek prose writer and the author of *Pápissa Ioánna (Pope Joan)*.

158 *retsina*   Resin-flavored wine.

158 *Trikoupis*   Harilaos Trikoupis (1832–96), a Greek prime minister.

159 *Rigas's organization*   Rigas Pheraios (1757–98) was one of the founders of the Philiki Etairia. He was born in Thessaly and lived in Constantinople and later in Vienna.

173 *the commanding poet*   Dionysios Solomos (1798–1857), the most renowned Zakynthian poet. The first two verses of his "Hymn to Liberty" became the Greek national anthem during the reign of George I.

180 *Porto Heli*   Located on the eastern coast of the Peloponnesus, near the island of Spetses.

181 *Romaic*   That is, Greek. "Romaic" is often juxtaposed to "Hellenic," the latter implying classical and classicizing and the former referring primarily to the indigenous Greek culture, including its Byzantine and Ottoman past.

193   The author's notes in this section appear at the end of the novel in the original Greek edition. The translator's additions, such as English translations of Greek titles and verses, appear in square brackets.